HORRiD HENRY'S
HOUSE OF HORRORS

Francesca Simon

HORRiD HENRY'S HOUSE of HORRORS

Illustrated by Tony Ross

Orion
Children's Books

For Marvellous Martin, without whom Horrid Henry
would have never happened

This collection first published in Great Britain in 2008
by Orion Children's Books
a division of the Orion Publishing Group Ltd
Orion House
5 Upper St Martin's Lane
London WC2H 9EA
An Hachette Livre UK Company

3 5 7 9 10 8 6 4 2

The Orion Publishing Group's policy is to use papers
that are natural, renewable and recyclable products and
made from wood grown in sustainable forests. The logging
and manufacturing processes are expected to conform to
the environmental regulations of the country of origin.

A catalogue record for this book
is available from the British Library.

ISBN 978 1 84255 649 8

Printed in Italy by Printer Trento

www.horridhenry.co.uk
www.orionbooks.co.uk

Contents

HEROIC HENRY'S BEST PICTURES

Grandma

Dog

Peter

Great-Aunt Greta

Rich Aunt Ruby

Mum

Dad

Stuck-up Steve

HORRiD HENRY'S CAR JOURNEY

'Henry! We're waiting!'

'Henry! Get down here!'

'Henry! I'm warning you!'

Horrid Henry sat on his bed and scowled. His mean, horrible parents could warn him all they liked. He wasn't moving.

'Henry! We're going to be late,' yelled Mum.

'Good!' shouted Henry.

'Henry! This is your final warning,' yelled Dad.

'I don't want to go to Polly's!' screamed Henry. 'I want to go to Ralph's birthday party.'

Mum stomped upstairs.

'Well you can't,' said Mum. 'You're coming to the christening, and that's that.'

'NO!' screeched Henry. 'I hate Polly, I hate babies, and I hate you!'

Henry had been a page-boy at the wedding of his cousin, Prissy Polly, when she'd married Pimply Paul. Now they had a prissy, pimply baby, Vomiting Vera.

Henry had met Vera once before. She'd thrown up all over him. Henry had hoped never to see her again until she was grown up and behind bars, but no such luck. He had to go and watch her be dunked in a vat of water, on the same day that Ralph was having a birthday party at Goo-Shooter World. Henry had been

longing for ages to go to Goo-Shooter World. Today was his chance. His only chance. But no. Everything was ruined.

Perfect Peter poked his head round the door.

'*I'm* all ready, Mum,' said Perfect Peter. His shoes were polished, his teeth were brushed, and his hair neatly combed. 'I know how annoying it is to be kept waiting when you're in a rush.'

'Thank you, darling Peter,' said Mum. 'At least *one* of my children knows how to behave.'

Horrid Henry roared and attacked. He was a swooping vulture digging his claws into a dead mouse.

'AAAAAAAAAEEEEEE!'

squealed Peter.

'Stop being horrid, Henry!' said Mum.

'No one told me it was today!' screeched Henry.

'Yes we did,' said Mum. 'But you weren't paying attention.'

'As usual,' said Dad.

'*I* knew we were going,' said Peter.

'I DON'T WANT TO GO TO POLLY'S!' screamed Henry. 'I want to go to Ralph's!'

'Get in the car – NOW!' said Dad.

'Or no TV for a year!' said Mum.

Eeek! Horrid Henry stopped wailing. No TV for a

year. Anything was better than that.

Grimly, he stomped down the stairs and out of the front door. They wanted him in the car. They'd have him in the car.

'Don't slam the door,' said Mum.

Slam!

Horrid Henry pushed Peter away from the car door and scrambled for the right-hand side behind the driver. Perfect Peter grabbed his legs and tried to climb over him.

Victory! Henry got there first.

13

Henry liked sitting on the right-hand side so he could watch the speedometer.

Peter liked sitting on the right-hand side so he could watch the speedometer.

'Mum,' said Peter. 'It's my turn to sit on the right.'

'No it isn't,' said Henry. 'It's mine.'

'Mine!'

'Mine!'

'We haven't even left and already you're fighting?' said Dad.

'You'll take turns,' said Mum. 'You can swap after we stop.'

Vroom.
Vroom.

Dad started the car.

The doors locked.

Horrid Henry was trapped.

But wait. Was there a glimmer of hope? Was there a teeny tiny chance? What was it Mum always said when he and Peter were squabbling in the car? 'If you don't stop fighting I'm going to turn around and go home!' And wasn't home just exactly where he wanted to be? All he had to do was to do what he did best.

'Could I have a story tape please?' said Perfect Peter.

'No! I want a music tape,' said Horrid Henry.

'I want "Mouse Goes to Town",' said Peter.

'I want "Driller Cannibals' Greatest Hits",' said Henry.

'Story!'

'Music!'

'Story!'

'Music!'

SMACK! SMACK!

'WAAAAAAA!'

'Stop it, Henry,' said Mum.

'Tell Peter to leave me alone!' screamed Henry.

'Tell Henry to leave *me* alone!' screamed Peter.

'Leave each other alone,' said Mum.

Horrid Henry glared at Perfect Peter.

Perfect Peter glared at Horrid Henry.

Horrid Henry stretched. Slowly, steadily, centimetre by centimetre, he spread out into Peter's area.

'Henry's on my side!'

'No I'm not!'

'Henry, leave Peter alone,' said Dad. 'I mean it.'

'I'm not doing anything,' said Henry. 'Are we there yet?'

'No,' said Dad.

Thirty seconds passed.

'Are we there yet?' said Horrid Henry.

'No!' said Mum.

'Are we there yet?' said Horrid Henry.

'NO!' screamed Mum and Dad.

'We only left ten minutes ago,' said Dad.

Ten minutes! Horrid Henry felt as if they'd been travelling for hours.

'Are we a quarter of the way there yet?'

'NO!'

'Are we halfway there yet?'

'NO!!'

'How much longer until we're halfway there?'

'Stop it, Henry!' screamed Mum.

'You're driving me crazy!' screamed Dad. 'Now be quiet and leave us alone.'

Henry sighed. Boy, was this boring. Why didn't they have a decent car, with built-in video games, movies, and jacuzzi? That's just what he'd have, when he was king.

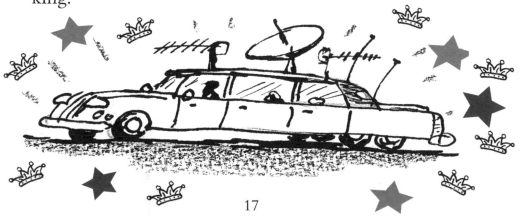

Softly, he started to hum under his breath.

'Henry's humming!'

'Stop being horrid, Henry!'

'I'm not doing anything,' protested Henry. He lifted his foot.

'MUM!' squealed Peter. 'Henry's kicking me.'

'Are you kicking him, Henry?'

'Not yet,' muttered Henry. Then he screamed.

'Mum! Peter's looking out of my window!'

'Dad! Henry's looking out of *my* window.'

'Peter breathed on me.'

'Henry's breathing loud on purpose.'

'Peter's on my side!'

'Henry's staring at me.'

'Tell him to stop!' screamed Henry and Peter.

Mum's face was red.

Dad's face was red.

'That's it!' screamed Dad.

'I can't take this any more!' screamed Mum.

Yes! thought Henry. We're going to turn back!

But instead of turning round, the car screeched to a halt at the motorway services.

'We're going to take a break,' said Mum. She looked exhausted.

'Who needs a wee?' said Dad. He looked even worse.

'Me,' said Peter.

'Henry?'

'No,' said Henry. He wasn't a baby. He knew when he needed a wee and he didn't need one now.

'This is our only stop, Henry,' said Mum. 'I think you should go.'

'NO!' screamed Henry. Several people looked up. 'I'll wait in the car.'

Mum and Dad were too tired to argue. They disappeared into the services with Peter.

Rats. Despite his best efforts, it looked like Mum and Dad were going to carry on. Well, if he couldn't make them turn back, maybe he could *delay* them? Somehow? Suddenly Henry had a wonderful, spectacular idea. It couldn't be easier, and it was guaranteed to work. He'd miss the christening!

Mum, Dad, and Peter got back in the car. Mum drove off.

'I need a wee,' said Henry.

'Not now, Henry.'

'I NEED A WEE!' screamed Henry. 'NOW!'

Mum headed back to the services.

Dad and Henry went to the toilets.

'I'll wait for you outside,' said Dad. 'Hurry up or we'll be late.'

Late! What a lovely word.

Henry went into the toilet and locked the door. Then he waited. And waited. And waited.

Finally, he heard Dad's grumpy voice.

'Henry? Have you fallen in?'

Henry rattled the door.

'I'm locked in,' said Henry. 'The door's stuck. I can't get out.'

'Try, Henry,' pleaded Dad.

'I have,' said Henry. 'I guess they'll have to break the door down.'

That should take a few hours. He settled himself on the toilet seat and got out a comic.

'Or you could just crawl underneath the partition into the next stall,' said Dad.

Aaargghh. Henry could have burst into tears. Wasn't it just his rotten luck to try to get locked in a toilet which had gaps on the sides? Henry didn't much fancy wriggling round on the cold floor. Sighing, he gave the stall door a tug and opened it.

Horrid Henry sat in silence for the rest of the trip. He was so depressed he didn't even protest when Peter demanded his turn on the right. Plus, he felt carsick.

Henry rolled down his window.

'Mum!' said Peter. 'I'm cold.'

Dad turned the heat on.

'Having the heat on makes me feel sick,' said Henry.

'I'm going to be sick!' whimpered Peter.

'I'm going to be sick,' whined Henry.

'But we're almost there,' screeched Mum. 'Can't you hold on until –'

Bleecccchh.

Peter threw up all over Mum.

Bleecccchh.

Henry threw up all over Dad.

The car pulled into the driveway.

Mum and Dad staggered out of the car to Polly's front door.

'We survived,' said Mum, mopping her dress.

'Thank God that's over,' said Dad, mopping his shirt.

Horrid Henry scuffed his feet sadly behind them. Despite all his hard work, he'd lost the battle. While Rude Ralph and Dizzy Dave and Jolly Josh were dashing about spraying each other with green goo later this afternoon he'd be

stuck at a boring party with lots of grown-ups yak yak yakking. Oh misery!

Ding dong.

The door opened. It was Prissy Polly. She was in her bathrobe and slippers. She carried a stinky, smelly, wailing baby over her shoulder. Pimply Paul followed.

He was wearing a filthy T-shirt with sick down the front.

'Eeeek,' squeaked Polly.

Mum tried to look as if she had not been through hell and barely lived to tell the tale.

'We're here!' said Mum brightly.
'How's the lovely baby?'

'Too prissy,' said Polly.

'Too pimply,' said Paul.

Polly and Paul looked at Mum and Dad.

'What are you doing here?' said Polly finally.

'We're here for the christening,' said Mum.

'Vera's christening?' said Polly.

'It's *next* weekend,' said Paul.

Mum looked like she wanted to sag to the floor.

Dad looked like he wanted to sag beside her.

'We've come on the wrong day?' whispered Mum.

'You mean, we have to go and come back?' whispered Dad.

'Yes,' said Polly.

'Oh no,' said Mum.

'Oh no,' said Dad.

'Bleecccch,' vomited Vera.

'Eeeek!' wailed Polly. 'Gotta go.'

She slammed the door.

'You mean, we can go home?' said Henry. 'Now?'

'Yes,' whispered Mum.

'Whoopee!' screamed Henry. 'Hang on, Ralph, here I come!'

Top tips to torment fellow passengers

1. Breathe loudly.
2. If there are three or more children, fight to get a window seat. If there are two children, fight to sit behind the driver so you can watch the speedometer.
3. Hum.
4. Ask 'Are we there yet?' every 30 seconds.
5. Get carsick.

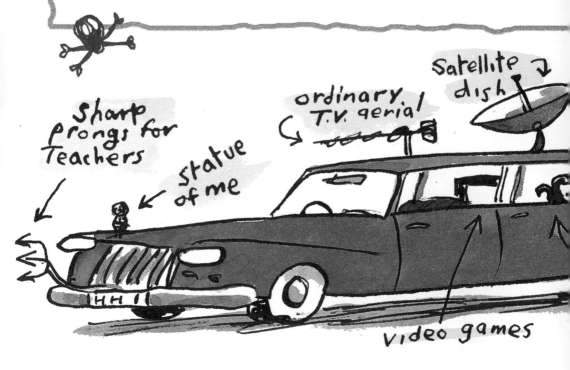

Sharp prongs for Teachers

statue of me

ordinary T.V. aerial

Satellite dish

video games

6. Make sure you take up as much room as possible. Steal as much space from your brother and sister as you can.
7. Demand lots of loo stops.
8. Fight about every CD. You only want the one someone else is listening to.
9. Get crumbs everywhere.
10. Fall asleep the moment you arrive.

acuzzi

Boot full of toys

Spare toys

Spare food, (mainly sweets)

hocolate fountain

HORRID HENRY'S DREAM CAR

HORRID HENRY
RUNS AWAY

orrid Henry was not having a good day. His younger brother, Perfect Peter, had grabbed the hammock first and wouldn't get out. Then Mum had ordered him to tidy his room just when he was watching *Rapper Zapper* on TV. And now Dad was yelling at him.

'What's the meaning of this letter, Henry?' shouted Dad.

'What letter?' snapped Henry. He was sick and tired of being nagged at.

'You know perfectly well what letter!' said Mum. 'The letter from Miss Battle-Axe. The third this week.'

Oh, *that* letter.

Dear Henry's Parents,
I am Sorry to tell you that today Henry:
Poked William
Tripped Linda
Shoved Dave
Pinched Andrew
Made rude noises, chewed gum,
and would not stop talking in class
Yours Sincerely,
Boudicca Battle-Axe

Henry scowled.

'Can I help it if I have to burp?'

'And what about all the children you hurt?' said Dad.

'I hardly touched William. Linda got in my way, and Dave and Andrew annoyed me,' said Henry. What a big fuss over nothing.

'Right,' said Dad. 'I am very disappointed with you. No TV, no comics and no sweets for a week.'

'A WEEK!' screamed Henry. 'For giving someone a little tap? It's not fair!'

'What about *my* letter?' said Peter.

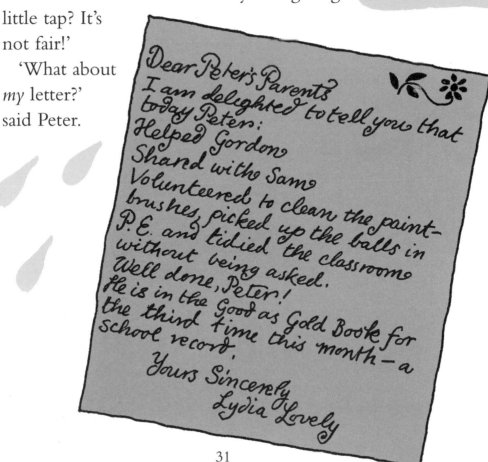

Dear Peter's Parents,
I am delighted to tell you that today Peter:
Helped Gordon
Shared with Sam
Volunteered to clean the paint-brushes, picked up the balls in P.E. and tidied the classroom without being asked.
Well done, Peter!
He is in the Good as Gold Book for the third time this month — a school record,
Yours Sincerely
Lydia Lovely

Dad glowed. 'At least *one* child in this family knows how to behave.'

Peter smiled modestly.

'You really should think more about other people, Henry,' said Peter. 'Then maybe one day *you'll* be in the Good as Gold Book.'

Horrid Henry snarled and leapt on Peter. He was primordial slime oozing over a trapped insect.

'Yeowww!' howled Peter.

'Stop it, Henry!' shouted Mum. 'Go straight to your room. NOW!'

Horrid Henry stomped upstairs to his bedroom and slammed the door.

'That's it!' screamed Henry. 'No one in this family likes me so I'm leaving!'

He'd show his horrible parents. He would run away to the jungle. He would fight giant snakes, crush crocodiles and paddle alone up piranha-infested rivers, hacking

his way through the vines. And he'd never ever come back. Then they'd be sorry. Serve them right for being so mean to him.

He could see them now. 'If only we'd been nicer to Henry', Dad would cry. 'Yes, such a lovely boy,' Mum would sob. 'Why oh why were we so cruel to him? If only Henry would come home he could always have the hammock,' Peter would whimper. 'Why was I so selfish?'

Shame really, thought Henry, dragging his suitcase from under the bed, that I won't be here to see them all wailing and gnashing their teeth.

Right, he thought, I'll only pack things I absolutely need. Lean and mean was the motto of Heroic Henry, Jungle Explorer.

Henry surveyed his room. What couldn't he live without?

He couldn't leave his Grisly Grub box and Dungeon Drink kit. Into the bag went the box and the kit. His Super Soaker 2000 water blaster would definitely come in handy in the wild. And of course, lots of games in case he got bored fighting panthers.

Comics? Henry considered … definitely. He stuffed a big stack in his bag. A few packets of crisps and some sweets would be good. And the box of Day-Glo slime. Henry certainly didn't want Peter getting his sticky fingers on his precious slime. Mr Kill? Nah! Mr Kill wouldn't be any use where he was going.

Perfect, thought Henry. Then he closed the bulging case. It would not shut. Very reluctantly Henry took out one comic and his football. There, he thought. He'd be off at dawn. And wouldn't they be sorry.

Tweet tweet.

Heroic Henry, Jungle Explorer, opened his eyes and leapt out of bed. The early birds were chirping. It was time to go. He flung on his jungle gear, then sneaked into Peter's room. He crept over to Peter's bed and pinched him.

'Wha–wha,' muttered Peter.

'Shut up and listen,' whispered Henry fiercely. 'I'm running away from home. If you tell anyone I've gone you'll be really sorry. In fact, you'll be dead.'

'I won't tell,' squeaked Peter.

'Good,' said Henry. 'And don't you dare touch anything in my room either.'

Horrid Henry crept down the stairs.

His suitcase clunked behind him. Henry froze. But no sound came from Mum and Dad's room.

At last Henry was safely down the stairs. Quietly he opened the back door and slipped into the misty garden.

He was outside. He was free! Goodbye civilization, thought Henry. Soon he'd be steaming down the Congo in search of adventure.

Of course I'll need a new name, thought Henry, as he began his long trek. To stop Mum and Dad tracking me down. Henry Intrepid sounded good. Piranha Pirate also had a nice ring. And I'll need to disguise myself too, thought Henry. He'd wait until he got to the jungle for that. He stole a quick glance behind him. No search party was after him so far.

Henry walked, and walked, and walked. His suitcase got heavier, and heavier, and heavier.

Phew! Henry was getting a bit tired dragging that case.

I feel like I've been travelling for miles, thought Henry. I think I'll stop and have a little rest at that secret hideaway. No one will find me there.

Horrid Henry clambered into the treehouse and stepped on something squishy.

'AHHH!' screamed Henry.

'AHHH!' screamed the Squishy Thing.

'What are *you* doing here?' snapped Horrid Henry.

'What are *you* doing here?' snapped Moody Margaret.

'I've run away from home, if you must know,' said Henry.

'So have I, and this is *my* treehouse,' said Margaret. 'Go away.'

'I can sit here if I want to,' said Henry, sitting down on Margaret's sleeping bag.

'Ouch! Get off my leg,' said Margaret, pushing him off.

'And don't think for a minute I'll let you come with me,' said Henry.

'You can't come with me, either,' said Margaret. 'So where are *you* going?'

'The Congo,' said Henry. He didn't know for sure exactly where that was, but he'd find it.

'Yuck,' said Margaret. 'Who'd want to go *there*? I'm going somewhere *much* better.'

'Where, smarty pants?' asked Henry. He eyed Margaret's rather plentiful stash of biscuits.

'Susan's house,' said Margaret.

Henry snorted.

'Susan's house? That's not running away.'

'It is too,' said Margaret.

''Tisn't.'

''Tis.'

''Tisn't.'

''Tis. And I slept here all night,' said Margaret.
'Where did *you* sleep?'

Henry eyed the distance between himself and
Margaret's biscuits. Whistling nonchalantly, Henry
stared in the opposite direction. Then, quick as a flash –
SNATCH!

Henry grabbed a handful of biscuits and stuffed
them in his mouth.

'Hey, that's my running-away food,' said Margaret.

'Not any more,' said Henry, snickering.

'Right,' said Margaret. She grabbed his case and
opened it. Then she hooted with laughter.

'That's all the food you brought?' she sneered. 'I'd like to see you get to the jungle with that. And all those comics! I bet you didn't even bring a map.'

'Oh yeah,' said Henry. 'What did *you* bring?'

Margaret opened her suitcase. Henry snorted with laughter.

'Clothes! I don't need clothes in the jungle. And anyway, *I* thought of running away first,' jeered Henry.

'Didn't,' said Margaret.

'Did,' said Henry.

'I'm going to tell your mother where you are,' said Margaret, 'and then you'll be in big trouble.'

'If you dare,' said Henry, 'I'll … I'll go straight over and tell yours. And I'll tell her you slept here last night. Won't you be in trouble then? In fact I'll go and tell her right now.'

'I'll tell yours first,' said Margaret.

They stood up, glaring at each other.

A faint, familiar smell drifted into the treehouse. It smelled like someone cooking.

Henry sniffed.

'What's that smell?'

Margaret sniffed.

'Pancakes,' she said.

Pancakes! Only Henry's favourite breakfast.

'Whose house?'

Margaret sniffed again.

'Yours,' she said sadly.

Yummy! Dad usually only made pancakes on special occasions. What could be happening? Then Henry had a terrible thought. Could it be … they were *celebrating* his departure?

How dare they? Well, he'd soon put a stop to that.

Henry clambered out of the treehouse and ran home.

'Mum! Dad! I'm back!' he shouted. 'Where are my pancakes?'

'They're all gone,' said Mum.

All gone!

'Why didn't you call me?' said Henry. 'You know I love pancakes.'

'We did call you,' said Mum, 'but you didn't come down. We thought you didn't want any.'

'But I wasn't here,' wailed Henry. He glared at Peter. Perfect Peter went on eating his pancakes a little faster, his arm protecting his plate.

'Peter knew I wasn't here,' said Henry. Then he lunged for Peter's plate. Peter screamed and held on tight.

'Henry said he'd kill me if I told so I didn't,' shrieked Peter.

'Henry, let go of that plate and don't be so horrid to your brother!' said Dad.

Henry let go. There was only half a pancake left anyway and it had Peter's yucky germs all over it.

Dad sighed.

'All right, I'll make another batch,' he said, getting up.

Henry was very surprised.

'Thanks, Dad,' said Henry. He sat down at the table.

A big steaming stack of pancakes arrived. Henry poured lashings of maple syrup on top, then stuffed a huge forkful of buttery pancakes into his mouth.

Yummy!

He'd head for the Congo tomorrow.

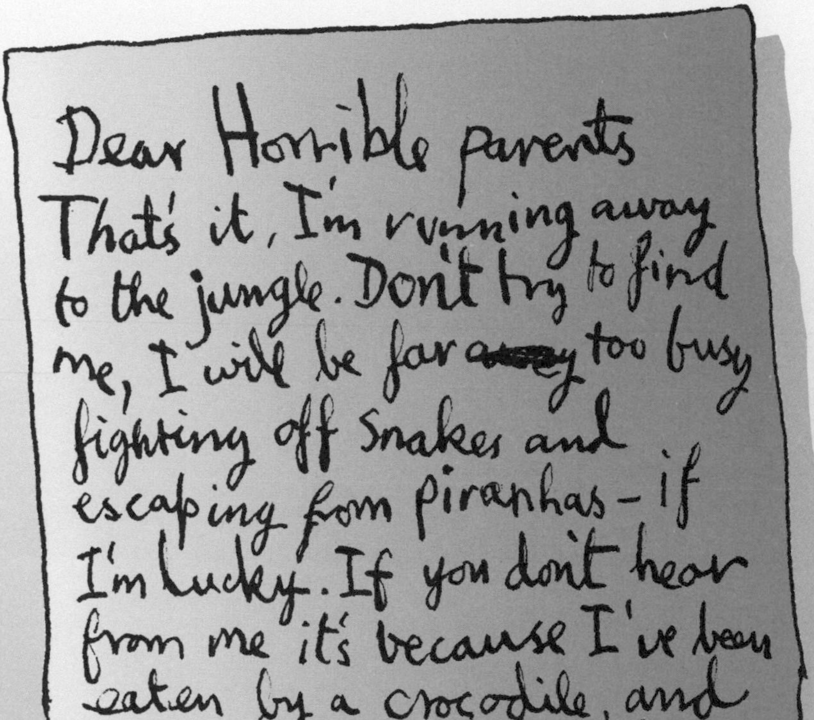

Dear Horrible parents

That's it, I'm running away to the jungle. Don't try to find me, I will be far ~~away~~ too busy fighting off snakes and escaping fom piranhas – if I'm lucky. If you don't hear from me it's because I've been eaten by a crocodile, and that will be all **YOUR** fault for being so mean to me.

Henry

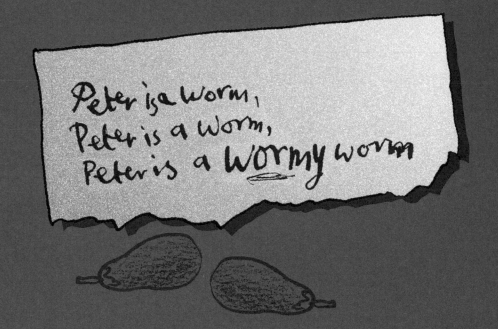

HORRID HENRY EATS A VEGETABLE

'Ugggh! Gross! Yuck! Bleeeeeech!'

Horrid Henry glared at the horrible, disgusting food slithering on his plate. Globby slobby blobs. Bumpy lumps. Rubbery blubbery globules of glop.

'Ugggh!'

How Dad and Mum and Peter could eat this swill without throwing up was amazing. Henry poked at the white, knobbly clump. It looked like brains. It felt like brains. Maybe it was . . .

Ewwwwwwww.

Horrid Henry pushed away his plate.
'I can't eat this,' moaned Henry. 'I'll be sick!'
'Henry! Cauliflower cheese is delicious,' said Mum.
'And nutritious,' said Dad.
'I love it,' said Perfect Peter. 'Can I have seconds?'

'It's nice to know *someone* appreciates my cooking,' said Dad. He frowned at Henry.

'But I hate vegetables,' said Henry. Yuck. Vegetables were so . . . healthy. And tasted so . . . vegetably. 'I want pizza!'

'Well, you can't have it,' said Dad.

'Ralph has pizza and chips every night at *his* house,' said Henry. 'And Graham *never* has to eat vegetables.'

'I don't care what Ralph and Graham eat,' said Mum.

'You've got to eat more vegetables,' said Dad.

'I eat loads of vegetables,' said Henry.

'Name one,' said Dad.

'Crisps,' said Henry.

'Crisps aren't vegetables, are they, Mum?' said Perfect Peter.

'No,' said Mum. 'Go on, Henry.'

'Ketchup,' said Henry.

'Ketchup is not a vegetable,' said Dad.

'It's impossible cooking for you,' said Mum.

'You're such a picky eater,' said Dad.

'I eat loads of things,' said Henry.

'Like what?' said Dad.

'Chips. Crisps. Burgers. Pizza. Chocolate. Sweets. Cake. Biscuits. Loads of food,' said Horrid Henry.

'That's not very healthy, Henry,' said Perfect Peter. 'You haven't said any fruit or vegetables.'

'So?' said Henry. 'Mind your own business, Toad.'

'Henry called me Toad,' wailed Peter.

'Ribbet. Ribbet,' croaked Horrid Henry.

'Don't be horrid, Henry,' snapped Dad.

'You can't go on eating so unhealthily,' said Mum.

'Agreed,' said Dad.

Uh oh, thought Henry. Here it comes. Nag nag nag. If there were prizes for best naggers Mum and Dad would win every time.

'I'll make a deal with you, Henry,' said Mum.

'What?' said Henry suspiciously. Mum and Dad's 'deals' usually involved his doing something horrible, for a pathetic reward. Well no way was he falling for that again.

'If you eat all your vegetables for five nights in a row, we'll take you to Gobble and Go.'

Henry's heart missed a beat. Gobble and Go! Gobble and Go! Only Henry's favourite restaurant in the whole wide world. Their motto: 'The chips just keep on coming!' shone forth from a purple neon sign. Music blared from twenty loudspeakers. Each table had its own TV. You could watch the chefs heat up your food in a giant microwave. Best of all, grownups never wanted to hang about for hours and chat. You ordered, gobbled, and left. Heaven.

And what fantastic food! Jumbo burgers. Huge pizzas. Lakes of ketchup. As many chips as you could eat. Fifty-two different ice creams. And not a vegetable in sight.

For some reason Mum and Dad hated Gobble and Go. They'd taken him once, and sworn they would never go again.

And now, unbelievably, Mum was offering.

'Deal!' shouted Henry, in case she changed her mind.

'So we're agreed,' said Mum. 'You eat your vegetables every night for five nights, and then we'll go.'

'Sure. Whatever,' said Horrid Henry eagerly. He'd agree to anything for a meal at Gobble and Go. He'd agree to dance naked down the street singing 'Hallelujah! I'm a nudie!' for the chance to eat at Gobble and Go.

Perfect Peter stopped eating his cauliflower. He didn't look very happy.

'I always eat *my* vegetables,' said Peter. 'What's my reward?'

'Health,' said Mum.

 ## String beans.

'Mum, Henry hasn't eaten any beans yet,' said Peter.

'I have too,' lied Henry.

'No you haven't,' said Peter. 'I've been watching.'

'Shut up, Peter,' said Henry.

'Mum!' wailed Peter. 'Henry told me to shut up.'

'Don't tell your brother to shut up,' said Mum.

'It's rude,' said Dad. 'Now eat your veg.'

Horrid Henry glared at his plate, teeming with slimy string beans. Just like a bunch of green worms, he thought. Yuck.

He must have been mad agreeing to eat vegetables for five nights in a row. He'd be poisoned before day three. Then they'd be sorry. 'How could we have been so cruel?' Mum would shriek. 'We've killed our own son,' Dad would moan. 'Why oh why did we make him eat his greens?' they would sob.

Too bad he'd be dead so he couldn't scream, 'I told you so!'.

'We have a deal, Henry,' said Dad.

'I know,' snapped Henry.

He cut off the teeniest, tiniest bit of string bean he could.

'Go on,' said Mum.

Slowly, Horrid Henry lifted his fork and put the poison in his mouth.

Aaaarrrgggghhhhh! What a horrible taste!

Henry spat and spluttered as the sickening sliver of string bean stuck in his throat.

'Water!' he gasped.

Perfect Peter speared several beans and popped them in his mouth.

'Great string beans, Dad,' said Peter. 'So crispy and crunchy.'

'Have mine if you like them so much,' muttered Henry.

'I want to see you eat every one of those string beans,' said Dad. 'Or no Gobble and Go.'

Horrid Henry scowled. No way was he eating another mouthful. The taste was too horrible. But, oh,

Gobble and Go. Those burgers! Those chips! Those TVs!

There had to be another way. Surely he, King Henry the Horrible, could defeat a plate of greens?

Horrid Henry worked out his battle plan. It was dangerous. It was risky. But what choice did he have?

First, he had to distract the enemy.

'You know, Mum,' said Henry, pretending to chew, 'you were right. These beans *are* very tasty.'

Mum beamed.

Dad beamed.

'I told you you'd like them if you tried them,' said Mum.

Henry pretended to swallow, then speared another bean. He pushed it round his plate.

Mum got up to refill the water jug. Dad turned to speak to her. Now was his chance!

Horrid Henry stretched out his foot under the table and lightly tickled Peter's leg.

'Look out, Peter, there's a spider on your leg.'

55

'Where?' squealed Peter, looking frantically under the table.

Leap! Plop!

Henry's beans hopped onto Peter's plate.

Peter raised his head.

'I don't see any spider,' said Peter.

'I knocked it off,' mumbled Henry, pretending to chew vigorously.

Then Peter saw his plate, piled high with string beans.

'Ooh,' said Peter, 'lucky me! I thought I'd finished!'

Tee hee, thought Horrid Henry.

Broccoli.

Plip!

A piece of Henry's broccoli 'accidentally' fell on the floor. Henry kicked it under Peter's chair.

Plop! Another piece of Henry's broccoli fell. And another. And another.

Plip plop. Plip plop. Plip plop.

Soon the floor under Peter's chair was littered with broccoli bits.

'Mum!' said Henry. 'Peter's making a mess.'

'Don't be a telltale, Henry,' said Dad.

'He's always telling on *me*,' said Henry.

Dad checked under Peter's chair.

'Peter! Eat more carefully. You're not a baby any more.'

Ha ha ha thought Horrid Henry.

Peas.

Squish!

Henry flattened a pea under his knife.

Squash!

Henry flattened another one.

Squish. Squash. Squish. Squash.

Soon every pea was safely squished and hidden under Henry's knife.

'Great dinner, Dad,' said Horrid Henry. 'Especially the peas. I'll clear,' he added, carrying his plate to the sink and quickly rinsing his knife.

Dad beamed.

'Eating vegetables is making you helpful,' said Dad.

'Yes,' said Henry sweetly. 'It's great being helpful.'

Day 4 Cabbage.

Buzz. Buzzzzz.

'A fly landed on my cabbage!' shrieked Henry. He swatted the air with his hands. 'Where?' said Mum.

'There!' said Henry. He leapt out of his seat.
'Now it's on the fridge!'

'Buzz,' said Henry under his breath.

'I don't see any fly,' said Dad.

'Up there!' said Henry, pointing to the ceiling.

Mum looked up.

Dad looked up.

Peter looked up.

Henry dumped a handful of cabbage in the bin.
Then he sat back down at the table.

'Rats,' said Henry. 'I can't eat the rest of my cabbage
now, can I? Not after a filthy horrible disgusting fly has
walked all over it, spreading germs and dirt and poo
and—'

'All right all right,' said Dad. 'Leave the rest.'

I am a genius, thought Horrid Henry, smirking.
Only one more battle until – Vegetable Victory!

Day 5 Sprouts.

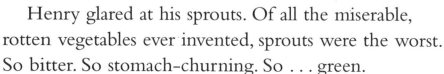

Mum ate her sprouts.

Dad ate his sprouts.

Peter ate his sprouts.

Henry glared at his sprouts. Of all the miserable, rotten vegetables ever invented, sprouts were the worst. So bitter. So stomach-churning. So . . . green.

But how to get rid of them? There was Peter's head, a tempting target. A very tempting target. Henry's sprout-flicking fingers itched. No, thought Horrid Henry. I can't blow it when I'm so close.

Should he throw them on the floor? Spit them in his napkin?

Or - Horrid Henry beamed. There was a little drawer in the table in front of Henry's chair. A perfect, Brussels sprout-sized drawer.

Henry eased it open. What could be simpler than stuffing a sprout or two inside while pretending to eat?

60

Soon the drawer was full. Henry's plate was empty.

'Look Mum! Look Dad!' screeched Henry. 'All gone!' Which was true, he thought gleefully.

'Well done, Henry,' said Dad.

'Well done, Henry,' said Peter.

'We'll take you to Gobble and Go tomorrow,' said Mum.

'Yippee!' screamed Horrid Henry.

Mum, Dad, Henry, and Peter walked up the street.

Mum, Dad, Henry, and Peter walked down the street.

Where was Gobble and Go, with its flashing neon sign, blaring music, and purple walls? They must have walked past it.

But how? Horrid Henry looked about wildly. It was impossible to miss Gobble and Go. You could see that neon sign for miles.

'It was right here,' said Horrid Henry.

But Gobble and Go was gone.

A new restaurant squatted in its place.

'The Virtuous Veggie,' read the sign. 'The all new vegetable restaurant!'

Horrid Henry gazed in horror at the menu posted outside.

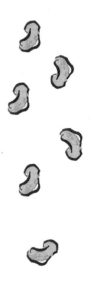

Cabbage Casserole
Pop-up Peas
Spinach Surprise
Sprouts a go-go
Choice of rhubarb or
broccoli ice cream

'Yummy!' said Perfect Peter.

'Look, Henry,' said Mum. 'It's serving all your new favourite vegetables.'

Horrid Henry opened his mouth to protest. Then he closed it. He knew when he was beaten.

I WANT!
GIMME!
BOY!
BOY!
BOY!

HORRID HENRY GOES SHOPPING

Horrid Henry stood in his bedroom up to his knees in clothes. The long sleeve stripy T-shirt came to his elbow. His trousers stopped halfway down his legs. Henry sucked in his tummy as hard as he could. Still the zip wouldn't zip.

'Nothing fits!' he screamed, yanking off the shirt and hurling it across the room. 'And my shoes hurt.'

'All right Henry, calm down,' said Mum. 'You've grown. We'll go out this afternoon and get you some new clothes and shoes.'

'NOOOOOOO!' shrieked Henry.

'NOOOOOOOOOOOOO!'

Horrid Henry hated shopping.

Correction: Horrid Henry loved shopping. He loved shopping for gigantic TVs, computer games, comics, toys, and sweets. Yet for some reason Horrid Henry's parents never wanted to go shopping for good stuff. Oh no. They shopped for hoover bags. Toothpaste. Spinach. Socks. Why oh why did he have such horrible parents? When he was grown-up he'd never set foot in

a supermarket. He'd only shop for TVs, computer games, and chocolate.

But shopping for clothes was even worse than heaving his heavy bones round the Happy Shopper Supermarket. Nothing was more boring than being dragged round miles and miles and miles of shops, filled with disgusting clothes only a mutant would ever want to wear, and then standing in a little room while Mum made you try on icky scratchy things you wouldn't be seen dead in if they were the last trousers on earth. It was horrible enough getting dressed once a day without doing it fifty times. Just thinking about trying on shirt after shirt after shirt made Horrid Henry want to scream.

'I'm not going shopping!' he howled, kicking the pile of clothes as viciously as he could. 'And you can't make me.'

'What's all this yelling?' demanded Dad.

'Henry needs new trousers,' said Mum grimly.

Dad went pale.

'Are you sure?'

'Yes,' said Mum. 'Take a look at him.'

Dad looked at Henry. Henry scowled.

'They're a *little* small, but not *that* bad,' said Dad.

'I can't breathe in these trousers!' shrieked Henry.

'That's why we're going shopping,' said Mum. 'And *I'll* take him.' Last time Dad had taken Henry shopping for socks and came back instead with three Hairy Hellhound CDs and a jumbo pack of Day-Glo slime.

'I don't know what came over me,' Dad had said, when Mum told him off.

'But why do *I* have to go?' said Henry. 'I don't want to waste my precious time shopping.'

'What about *my* precious time?' said Mum.

Henry scowled. Parents didn't have precious time. They were there to serve their children. New trousers should just magically appear, like clean clothes and packed lunches.

Mum's face brightened. 'Wait, I have an idea,' she beamed. She rushed out and came back with a large plastic bag. 'Here,' she said, pulling out a pair of bright red trousers, 'try these on.'

Henry looked at them suspiciously.

'Where are they from?'

'Aunt Ruby dropped off some of Steve's old clothes a few weeks ago. I'm sure we'll find something that fits you.'

Horrid Henry stared at Mum. Had she gone gaga? Was she actually suggesting that he should wear his horrible cousin's mouldy old shirts and pongy pants? Just imagine, putting his arms into the same stinky sleeves that Stuck-up Steve had slimed? Uggh!

'NO WAY!' screamed Henry, shuddering. 'I'm not wearing Steve's smelly old clothes. I'd catch rabies.'

'They're practically brand new,' said Mum.

'I don't care,' said Henry.

'But Henry,' said Perfect Peter. 'I always wear *your* hand-me-downs.'

'So?' snarled Henry.

'I don't mind wearing hand-me-downs,' said Perfect Peter. 'It saves so much money. You shouldn't be so selfish, Henry.'

'Quite right, Peter,' said Mum, smiling. 'At least *one* of my sons thinks about others.'

Horrid Henry pounced. He was a vampire sampling his supper.

'AAIIIEEEEEE!' squealed Peter.

'Stop that, Henry!' screamed Mum.

'Leave your brother alone!' screamed Dad.

Horrid Henry glared at Peter.

'Peter is a worm, Peter is a toad,' jeered Henry.

'Mum!' wailed Peter. 'Henry said I was a worm. And a toad.'

'Don't be horrid, Henry,' said Dad. 'Or no TV for a week. You have three choices. Wear Steve's old clothes. Wear your old clothes. Go shopping for new ones today.'

'Do we *have* to go today?' moaned Henry.

'Fine,' said Mum. 'We'll go tomorrow.'

'I don't want to go tomorrow,' wailed Henry. 'My weekend will be ruined.'

Mum glared at Henry.

'Then we'll go right now this minute.'

'**NO!**' screamed Horrid Henry.

'**YES!**' screamed Mum.

Several hours later, Mum and Henry walked into Mellow Mall. Mum already looked like she'd been crossing the Sahara desert without water for days. Serve her right for bringing me here, thought

Horrid Henry, scowling, as he scuffed his feet.

'Can't we go to Shop 'n' Drop?' whined Henry.
'Graham says they've got a win your weight in chocolate
competition.'

'No,' said Mum, dragging Henry into Zippy's
Department Store. 'We're here to get you some new
trousers and shoes. Now hurry up, we don't have all
day.'

Horrid Henry looked around. Wow! There was lots
of great stuff on display.

'I want the Hip-Hop Robots,' said Henry.

'No,' said Mum.

'I want the new
Supersoaker!'
screeched Henry.
'No,' said
Mum.

'I want a
Creepy
Crawly
lunchbox!'
'NO!' said
Mum, pulling
him into the
boys' clothing
department.

What, thought Horrid Henry grimly, is the point of
going shopping if you never buy anything?

'I want Root-a-Toot trainers with flashing red lights,'
said Henry. He could see himself now, strolling into
class, a bugle blasting and red light flashing every time
his feet hit the floor. Cool! He'd love to see Miss
Battle-Axe's face when
he exploded into class
wearing them.

'No,' said Mum,
shuddering.

'Oh please,' said
Henry.

'NO!' said Mum,
'we're here to buy
trousers and sensible
school shoes.'

'But I want Root-a-Toot trainers!' screamed Horrid
Henry. 'Why can't we buy what *I* want to buy? You're
the meanest mother in the world and I hate you!'

'Don't be horrid, Henry. Go and try these on,' said
Mum, grabbing a selection of hideous trousers and
revolting T-shirts. 'I'll keep looking.'

Horrid Henry sighed loudly and slumped towards
the dressing room. No one in the world suffered as
much as he did. Maybe he could hide between the
clothes racks and never come out.

Then something wonderful in the toy department next door caught his eye.

Whooa! A whole row of the new megalotronic animobotic robots with 213 programmable actions. Horrid Henry dumped the clothes and ran over to have a look. Oooh, the new Intergalactic Samurai Gorillas which launched real stinkbombs! And the latest Super Soakers! And deluxe Dungeon Drink kits with a celebrity chef recipe book! To say nothing of the Mega-Whirl Goo-Shooter which sprayed fluorescent goo for fifty metres in every direction. Wow!

Mum staggered into the dressing room with more clothes. 'Henry?' said Mum.

No reply.

'HENRY!' said Mum.

Still no reply.

Mum yanked open a dressing room door.

'Hen—'

'Excuse *me!*' yelped a bald man, standing in his underpants.

'Sorry,' said Mum, blushing bright pink. She dashed out of the changing room and scanned the shop floor.

Henry was gone.

Mum searched up the aisles.

No Henry.

Mum searched down the aisles.

Still no Henry.

Then Mum saw a tuft of hair sticking up behind the neon sign for Ballistic Bazooka Boomerangs. She marched over and hauled Henry away.

'I was just looking,' protested Henry.

Henry tried on one pair of trousers after another.

'No, no, no, no, no, no, no,' said Henry, kicking off the final pair. 'I hate all of them.'

'All right,' said Mum, grimly. 'We'll look somewhere else.'

Mum and Henry went to Top Trousers. They went to Cool Clothes. They went to Stomp in the Swamp. Nothing had been right.

'Too tight,' moaned Henry.

'Too itchy!'

'Too big!'

'Too small!'

'Too ugly!'

'Too red!'

'Too uncomfortable!'

'We're going to Tip-Top Togs,' said Mum wearily. 'The first thing that fits, we're buying.'

Mum staggered into the children's department and grabbed a pair of pink and green tartan trousers in Henry's size.

'Try these on,' she ordered. 'If they fit we're having them.'

Horrid Henry gazed in horror at the horrendous trousers.

'Those are girls' trousers!' he screamed.

'They are not,' said Mum.

'Are too!' shrieked Henry.

'I'm sick and tired of your excuses, Henry,' said Mum. 'Put them on or no pocket money for a year. I mean it.'

Horrid Henry put on the pink and green tartan trousers, puffing out his stomach as much as possible. Not even Mum would make him buy trousers that were too tight.

Oh no. The horrible trousers had an elastic waist. They would fit a mouse as easily as an elephant.

'And lots of room to grow,' said Mum brightly. 'You can wear them for years. Perfect.'

'NOOOOOOO!'

howled Henry. He flung himself on the floor kicking and screaming.

'NOOOOOOO!'
'They're GIRLS' trousers!!!'

'We're buying them,' said Mum. She gathered up the tartan trousers and stomped over to the till. She tried not to think about starting all over again trying to find a pair of shoes that Henry would wear.

A little girl in pigtails walked out of the dressing room, twirling in pink and green tartan trousers.

'I love them, Mummy!' she shrieked. 'Let's get three pairs.'

Horrid Henry stopped howling. He looked at Mum. Mum looked at Henry. Then they both looked at the pink and green tartan trousers Mum was carrying.

ROOT-A-TOOT!
ROOT-A-TOOT!
ROOT-A-TOOT!
TOOT! TOOT!

An earsplitting bugle blast shook the house. Flashing red lights bounced off the walls.

'What's that noise?' said Dad, covering his ears.

'What noise?' said Mum, pretending to read.

ROOT-A-TOOT!
ROOT-A-TOOT!
ROOT-A-TOOT!
TOOT! TOOT!

~~D~~ad stared at Mum.

'~~You~~ didn't,' said Dad. 'Not—Root-a-Toot trainers?'

~~Mum hi~~d her face in her hands.

'~~I don't kn~~ow what came over me,' said Mum.

79

What I need !!!!!!!!

10 pairs of Root-a-Toot trainers

Megalotronic Animobotic Robots
(plus attachments)

Creepy-Crawly lunchbox
and flask

Hairy Hellhound Greatest Hits

Mega-gigantic TV with
wraparound screen and
12 speakers

HORRID HENRY'S HOBBY

'Out of my way, worm!' shrieked Horrid Henry, pushing past his younger brother Perfect Peter and dashing into the kitchen.

'NO!' screamed Perfect Peter. He scrambled after Henry and clutched his leg.

'Get off me!' shouted Henry. He grabbed the unopened Sweet Tweet cereal box. 'Nah nah ne nah nah, I got it first.'

Perfect Peter lunged for the Sweet Tweet box and snatched it from Henry. 'But it's my turn!'

'No, mine!' shrieked Henry. He ripped open the top and stuck his hand inside.

'It's mine!' shrieked Peter. He ripped open the bottom.

A small wrapped toy fell to the floor.

Henry and Peter both lunged for it.

'Gimme that!' yelled Henry.

'But it's my turn to have it!' yelled Peter.

'Stop being horrid, Henry!' shouted Mum. 'Now give me that thing!'

Henry and Peter both held on tight.

'NO!' screamed Henry and Peter. 'IT'S MY TURN TO HAVE THE TOY!'

Horrid Henry and Perfect Peter both collected Gizmos from inside Sweet Tweet cereal boxes. So did everyone at their school. There were ten different coloured Gizmos to collect, from the common green to the rare gold. Both Henry and Peter had Gizmos of every colour. Except for one. Gold.

'Right,' said Mum, 'whose turn is it to get the toy?'

'MINE!' screamed Henry and Peter.

'He got the last one!' screeched Henry. 'Remember – he opened the new box and got the blue Gizmo.'

It was true that Perfect Peter had got the blue Gizmo – two boxes ago. But why should Peter get any? If he hadn't started collecting Gizmos to copy me, thought Henry resentfully, I'd get every single one.

'NO!' howled Peter. He burst into tears. 'Henry opened the last box.'

'Crybaby,' jeered Henry.

'Stop it,' said Peter.

'Stop it,' mimicked Henry.

'Mum, Henry's teasing me,' wailed Peter.

'I remember now,' said Mum. 'It's Peter's turn.'

'Thank you, Mum,' said Perfect Peter.

'It's not fair!' screamed Horrid Henry as Peter tore open the wrapping. There was a gold gleam.

'Oh my goodness,' gasped Peter. 'A gold Gizmo!'

Horrid Henry felt as if he'd been punched in the stomach. He stared at the glorious, glowing, golden Gizmo.

'It's not fair!' howled Henry. 'I want a gold Gizmo!'

'I'm sorry, Henry,' said Mum. 'It'll be your turn next.'

'But I want the gold one!' screamed Henry.

He leaped on Peter and yanked the Gizmo out of his hand. He was Hurricane Henry uprooting everything in his path.

'Helllllllp!'

howled Peter.

'Stop being horrid, Henry, or no more Gizmos for you!' shouted Mum. 'Now clean up this mess and get dressed.'

'NO!' howled Henry. He ran upstairs to his room, slamming the door behind him.

He had to have a gold Gizmo. He simply had to. No one at school had a gold one. Henry could see himself now, the centre of attention, everyone pushing and shoving just to get a look at his gold Gizmo. Henry could charge 20p a peek. Everyone would want

to see it and to hold it. Henry would be invited to every birthday party. Instead, Peter would be the star attraction. Henry gnashed his teeth just thinking about it.

But how could he get one? You couldn't buy Gizmos. You could only get them inside Sweet Tweet cereal boxes. Mum was so mean she made Henry and

Peter finish the old box before she'd buy a new one. Henry had eaten mountains of Sweet Tweet cereal to collect all his Gizmos. All that hard work would be in vain, unless he got a gold one.

He could, of course, steal Peter's. But Peter would be sure to notice, and Henry would be the chief suspect.

He could swap. Yes! He would offer Peter *two* greens! That was generous. In fact, that was really generous. But Peter hated doing swaps. For some reason he always thought Henry was trying to cheat him.

And then suddenly Henry had a brilliant, spectacular idea. True, it did involve a little tiny teensy weensy bit of trickery, but Henry's cause was just. *He'd* been collecting Gizmos far longer than Peter had. He deserved a gold one, and Peter didn't.

'So, you got a gold Gizmo,' said Henry, popping into Peter's room. 'I'm really sorry.'

Perfect Peter looked up from polishing his Gizmos. 'Why?' he said suspiciously. '*Everyone* wants a gold Gizmo.'

Horrid Henry looked sadly at Perfect Peter. 'Not any more. They're very unlucky, you know. Every single person who's got one has died horribly.'

Perfect Peter stared at Henry, then at his golden Gizmo.

'That's not true, Henry.'

'Yes it is.'

'No it isn't.'

Horrid Henry walked slowly around Peter's room. Every so often he made a little note in a notebook.

'Marbles, check. Three knights, check. Nature kit – nah. Coin collection, check.'

'What are you doing?' said Peter.

'Just looking round your stuff to see what I want when you're gone.'

'Stop it!' said Peter. 'You just made that up about gold Gizmos – didn't you?'

'No,' said Henry. 'It's in all the newspapers. There was the boy out walking his dog who fell into a pit of

molten lava. There was the girl who drowned in the loo, and then that poor boy who—'

'I don't want to die,' said Perfect Peter. He looked pale. 'What am I going to do?'

Henry paused. 'There's nothing you can do. Once you've got it you're sunk.'

Peter jumped up.

'I'll throw it away!'

'That wouldn't work,' said Henry. 'You'd still be jinxed. There's only one way out—'

'What?' said Perfect Peter.

'If you give the gold away to someone brave enough to take it, then the jinx passes to them.'

'But no one will take it from me!' wailed Peter.

'Tell you what,' said Henry. 'I'll take the risk.'

'Are you sure?' said Peter.

'Of course,' said Horrid Henry. 'You're my brother. You'd risk your life for me.'

'OK,' said Peter. He handed Henry the gold Gizmo. 'Thank you, Henry. You're the best brother in the world.'

'I know,' said Horrid Henry.

He actually had his very own gold Gizmo in his hand. It was his, fair and square. He couldn't wait to see Moody Margaret's face when he waved it in front of her. And Rude Ralph. He would be green with envy.

Then Perfect Peter burst into tears and ran downstairs.

'Mum!' he wailed. 'Henry's going to die! And it's all my fault.'

'What?' screeched Mum.

Uh oh, thought Henry. He clutched his treasure.

Mum stormed upstairs. She snatched the gold Gizmo from Henry.

'How could you be so horrid, Henry?' shouted Mum. 'No TV for a week! Poor Peter. Now get ready. We're going shopping.'

'NO!' howled Henry. 'I'm not going!'

Horrid Henry scowled as he followed Mum up and down the aisles of the Happy Shopper. He'd crashed the cart into some people so Mum wouldn't let him push it. Then she caught him filling the cart with crisps and fizzy drinks and made him put them all back. What a horrible rotten day this had turned out to be.

'Yum, cabbage,' said Perfect Peter. 'Could we get some?'

'Certainly,' said Mum.

'And sprouts, my favourite!' said Peter.

'Help yourself,' said Mum.

'I want sweets!' screamed Henry.

'No,' said Mum.

'I want doughnuts!' screamed Henry.

'No!' screamed Mum.

'There's nothing to eat here!' shrieked Henry.

'Stop being horrid, Henry,' hissed Mum. 'Everyone's looking.'

'I don't care.'

'Well I do,' said Mum. 'Now make yourself useful. Go and get a box of Sweet Tweets.'

'All right,' said Henry. Now was his chance to escape. Before Mum could stop him he grabbed a cart and whizzed off.

'Watch out for the racing driver!' squealed Henry.

Shoppers scattered as he zoomed down the aisle and screeched to a halt in front of the cereal section. There were the Sweet Tweets. A huge pile of them, in a display tower, under a twinkling sign saying, 'A free Gizmo in every box! Collect them all!'

Henry reached for a box and put it in his cart.

And then Horrid Henry stopped. What was the point of buying a whole box if it just contained another green Gizmo? Henry didn't think he could bear it. I'll just check what's inside, he thought. Then, if it *is* a green one, I'll be prepared for the disappointment.

Carefully, he opened the box and slipped his hand inside. Aha! There was the toy. He lifted it out, and held it up to the light. Rats! A green Gizmo, just what he'd feared.

But wait. There was bound to be a child out there longing for a green Gizmo to complete his collection just as much as Henry was longing for a gold. Wouldn't it be selfish and horrid of Henry to take a green he didn't need when it would make someone else so happy?

I'll just peek inside one more box, thought Horrid Henry, replacing the box he'd opened and reaching for another.

He tore it open. Red.

Hmmm, thought Henry. Red is surplus to requirements.

Another box opened. Blue.

95

Rip! Rip! Rip!

Green! Green! Blue!

I'll just try one more at the back, thought Henry.
He stood on tiptoe, and stretched as far as he could.
His hand reached inside the box and grabbed hold of
the toy.

The tower wobbled.

CRASH!

Horrid Henry sprawled on the ground. Henry was covered in Sweet Tweets. So was the floor. So were all the shoppers.

'HELP!'

screamed the manager, skidding in the mess. 'Whose horrid boy is this?'

Skid!

There was a very long silence.
'Mine,' whispered Mum.

Horrid Henry sat in the kitchen surrounded by boxes and boxes and boxes of Sweet Tweets. He'd be eating Sweet Tweets for breakfast, lunch and dinner for weeks. But it was worth it, thought Henry happily.

Banned for life from the Happy Shopper, how wonderful. He uncurled his hand to enjoy again the glint of gold.

Although he *had* noticed that Scrummy Yummies were offering a free Twizzle card in every box. Hmmmm, Twizzle cards.

THE HENRY MUSEUM

HORRID HENRY'S BATHTIME

orrid Henry loved baths.

He loved causing great big tidal waves.

He loved making bubble-bath beards and bubble-bath hats.

He loved staging battles with Yellow Duck and Snappy Croc. He loved diving for buried treasure, fighting sea monsters, and painting the walls with soapy suds.

But best of all, being in the bath meant Peter couldn't bother him, or wreck his games or get him into trouble.

Henry stretched out in the lovely warm water. The bubbles were piled high to overflowing, just as he liked.

SLOSH SLOSH SLOSH

A bucketload of soapy suds cascaded onto the floor. Yippee! The first tidal wave of the day. Good thing Mum wasn't around. But then what Mum didn't know wouldn't hurt her.

Now what to do first? A Croc and Duck fight? Or the killer tidal wave?

'Heh heh heh,' cackled Horrid Henry, 'watch your tail Yellow Duck, 'cause Snappy Croc is on the attack. Snap! Snap! Snap!'

Suddenly the bathroom door opened. A slimy toad slithered in.

'Oy, get out of here, Peter,' said Henry.

'Dad said we had to share a bath,' said Perfect Peter, taking off his shirt.

What?

'Liar!' screeched Horrid Henry. 'You are dead meat!' He reached for his Super Soaker. Henry was not allowed to use it in the house, but this was an emergency.

'AAARRRGGGHHH,'

squealed Peter as a jet of water hit him in the face.

Dad dashed in.

'Put that Super Soaker away or I'll confiscate it,' shouted Dad.

Henry's finger trembled on the trigger. Dad's red face was so tempting . . .

Henry could see it now. POW! Dad soaking wet. Dad screaming. Dad snatching the Super Soaker and throwing it in the rubbish and telling Henry no TV for ever . . .

Hmmm. Dad's red face was a little less tempting.

'Just look at this floor, Henry,' said Dad. 'What a waste of water.'

'It's not a waste,' said Horrid Henry, holding tight onto his Super Soaker in case Dad lunged, 'it's a tidal wave.'

'Too much water is being wasted in this house,' said Dad. 'From now on you and Peter will share a bath.'

Horrid Henry could not believe his ears. *Share* a bath? *Share* a bath with stupid smelly Peter?

'NOOOO,' wailed Henry.

'I don't mind sharing, Dad,' said Peter. 'We all have to do our bit to save water.'

'But Peter pees in the bath,' said Henry.

'I do not,' said Perfect Peter. 'Henry does.'

'Liar!'

'Liar!'

'And we'll be squashed!' wailed Henry. 'And he likes the bath too cold ! And he – '

'That's enough Henry,' said Dad. 'Now make room for Peter.'

Horrid Henry ducked his head under water. He was never coming back up. Never. Then they'd be sorry they made him share his bath with an ugly toad snotface telltale goody-goody poo breath . . .

GASP.

Horrid Henry came up for air.

'If you don't make room for Peter you'll be getting out now,' said Dad. 'And no TV for a week.'

Scowling, Horrid Henry moved his legs a fraction of an inch.

'Henry . . .' said Dad.

Horrid Henry moved his legs another fraction.

'I don't want to sit by the taps,' said Peter. 'They hurt my back.'

'Well I don't want to sit there either,' said Henry. 'And I was here first. I'm not moving.'

'Just get in, Peter,' said Dad.

Perfect Peter got in the bath and sat against the taps. His lower lip trembled.

Ha ha ha, thought Horrid Henry, stretching out his

legs. Peter was all squished at the yucky end of the bath. Good. Serve him right for ruining Henry's fun.

'Nah nah ne nah nah,' chortled Horrid Henry.

'Dad, the bath's too hot,' moaned Peter. 'I'm boiling.' Dad added cold water.

'Too cold!' screeched Horrid Henry. 'I'm freezing!' Dad added hot water.

'Too hot!' said Perfect Peter.

Dad sighed.

'New house rule: the person who sits by the taps decides the temperature,' said Dad, letting in a trickle of cold water. 'Now I don't want to hear another peep out of either of you,' he added, closing the door.

Horrid Henry could have punched himself. Why hadn't he thought of that? If he were by the taps *he'd* be the bath king.

'Move,' said Henry.

'No,' said Peter.

'I want to sit by the taps,' said Henry.

'Too bad,' said Peter. 'I'm not moving.'

'Make it hotter,' ordered Henry.

'No,' said Peter. 'I control the temperature because *I'm* sitting by the taps.'

'DAD!' shouted Henry. 'Peter wants the bath too cold!'

'MUM!' shouted Peter. 'Henry wants the bath too hot!'

'I'm freezing!'

'I'm boiling!'

'Be quiet both of you,' screamed Dad from the kitchen.

Horrid Henry glared at Peter.

Perfect Peter glared at Henry.

'Move your legs,' said Henry.

'I'm on my side,' said Peter.

Henry kicked him.

'No you're not,' said Henry.

Peter kicked him back.

Henry splashed him.

'Muuuuuuum!' shrieked Peter. 'Henry's being horrid.'

'Peter's being horrid!'

'Make him stop!' shouted Henry and Peter.

'AAARRRGGGHHH!'

screeched Peter.

'AAARRRGGGHHH!'

screeched Henry.

'Stop fighting!' screamed Mum.

Perfect Peter picked up Yellow Duck.

'Give me Yellow Duck,' hissed Henry.

'No,' said Peter.

'But it's my duck!'

'Mine!'

'WAAAAAAA!'

wailed Peter. 'Muuuuuuuum!'

Mum ran in. 'What's going on in here?'

'He hit me!' screeched Henry and Peter.

'That's it, both of you out,' said Mum.

'Bathtime, boys,' said Mum the next evening.

Horrid Henry raced upstairs. This time he'd make
sure he was the first one in. But when he reached the
bathroom, a terrible sight met his eyes. There was Peter,
already sitting at the tap end. Henry could practically
see the ice cubes floating on the freezing water.

Rats. Another bathtime ruined.

Henry stuck his toe in.

'It's too cold!' moaned Henry. 'And I don't want to
have a bath with Peter. I want my own bath.'

'Stop making a fuss and get in,' said Mum. 'And no
fighting. I'm leaving the door open.'

Horrid Henry got into the bath.

Eeeeek! He was turning into an icicle! Well, not for

long. He had a brilliant, spectacular plan.

'Stop making ripples,' hissed Horrid Henry. 'You have to keep the water smooth.'

'I am keeping the water smooth,' said Peter.

'Shh! Hold still.'

'Why?' said Peter.

'I wouldn't splash if I were you,' whispered Henry. '*It* doesn't like splashing.'

'Why are you whispering?' said Peter.

'Because there's a monster in the tub,' said Henry.

'No there isn't,' said Peter.

'It's the plughole monster,' said Horrid Henry. 'It sneaks up the drains, slithers through the plughole and – slurp! Down you go.'

'You big liar,' said Peter. He shifted slightly off the plughole.

Henry shrugged.

'It's up to you,' he said. 'Don't say I didn't warn you when the Plughole Monster sucks you down the drain!'

Peter scooted away from the plughole.

'MUUUUM!' he howled, jumping out of the bath.

Henry grabbed his spot, turned on the hot water, and stretched out. Ahhhh!

Peter continued to shriek.

'What's going on in here?' said Mum and Dad, bursting into the bathroom.

110

'Henry said I was going to get sucked down the plughole,' snivelled Peter.

'Don't be horrid, Henry,' said Mum. 'Get out of the bath this minute.'

'But – but . . .' said Horrid Henry.

'New house rules,' said Mum. 'From now on *I'll* run the bath and *I'll* decide the temperature.'

We'll see about that, thought Horrid Henry.

The next evening, Henry sneaked into the bathroom. A thin trickle of water dribbled from the tap. The bath was just starting to fill. He felt the water.

Brrr! Freezing cold. Just how he hated it. Peter must have fiddled with the temperature. Well, no way! Henry turned up the hot tap full blast. Hot water gushed into the bath. That's much better, thought Horrid Henry. He smiled and went downstairs.

From his bedroom, Peter heard Henry stomping from the bathroom. What was he up to? When the coast was clear, Peter tiptoed into the bathroom and dipped his fingers in the water. Oww! Boiling hot. Just how he hated it. Henry must have fiddled with the temperature:

Mum would *never* make it so hot. Peter turned up the cold tap full blast. Much better, thought Peter.

Mum and Dad were sitting in the kitchen drinking tea.

Mum smiled. 'It's lovely and quiet upstairs, isn't it?'

Dad smiled. 'I knew they'd be able to share a bath, in the end.'

Mum stopped smiling.

'Do you hear something?'

Dad listened.

'Leave me alone!' screamed Henry from the sitting room.

'You leave me alone!' screamed Peter.

'Just the usual,' said Dad.

'Didn't you put them in the bath?'

Dad stopped smiling. 'No. Didn't you?'

Mum looked at Dad.

Dad looked at Mum.

Plink! Plink! Plink!

112

Water began to drip from the ceiling.

'I think I hear – RUNNING WATER!' screamed Mum. She dashed up the stairs.

Dad ran after her.

Mum opened the bathroom door.

Water gushed from the bathroom, and roared down the stairs. **Slide! Slip!**

Mum landed on her bottom.

Plop!

Dad toppled into the bath.

Splash!

'It wasn't me!' screamed Henry.

'It wasn't me!' wailed Peter. Then he burst into tears.

'Mum!' wept Peter. 'I've been a bad boy.'

Snap! Snap!

Snappy Croc was defending his tail. Yellow Duck was twisting round to attack. Ka-boom!

Horrid Henry lay back in the bath and closed his eyes. Mum and Dad had decided to let Henry have baths on his own. To save water, they'd take showers.

HORRID HENRY RULES THE WAVES

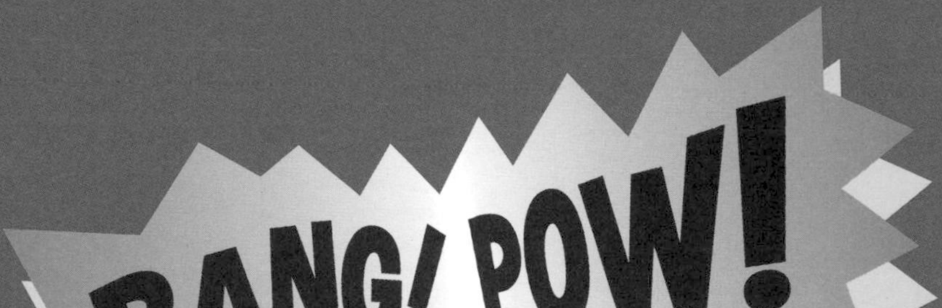
BANG! POW!

HORRID HENRY AND THE MEGA-MEAN TIME MACHINE

orrid Henry flicked the switch. The time machine whirred. Dials spun. Buttons pulsed. Latches locked. Horrid Henry, Time Traveller, was ready for blast off!

Now, where to go, where to go?

Dinosaurs, thought Henry. Yes! Henry loved dinosaurs. He would love to stalk a few Tyrannosaurus Rexes as they rampaged through the primordial jungle.

But what about King Arthur and the Knights of the Round Table? 'Arise, Sir Henry,' King Arthur would say, booting Lancelot out of his chair. 'Sure thing, King,' Sir Henry would reply, twirling his sword. 'Out of my way, worms!'

Or what about the siege of Troy? Heroic Henry, that's who he'd be, the fearless fighter dashing about doing daring deeds.

Tempting, thought Henry. Very tempting.

Wait a sec, what about visiting the future, where school was banned and parents had to do whatever their children told them? Where everyone had their own spaceship and ate sweets for dinner. And where King Henry the Horrible ruled supreme, chopping off the head of anyone who dared to say no to him.

To the future, thought Henry, setting the dial.

Henry braced himself for the jolt into hyperspace –

'Henry, it's my turn.'
Horrid Henry ignored the alien's whine.

'Henry! If you don't share I'm going to tell Mum.'

AAAARRRRGGGHHHHHH.

The Time Machine juddered to a halt. Henry climbed out.

'Go away, Peter,' said Henry. 'You're spoiling
everything.'

'But it's my turn.'

'GO AWAY!'

'Mum said we could *both* play with the box,' said
Peter. 'We could cut out windows, make a little house,
paint flowers – '

'NO!' screeched Henry.

'But . . . ' said Peter. He stood in the sitting room,
holding his scissors and crayons.

'Don't you touch my box!' hissed Henry.

'I will if I want to,' said Peter. 'And it's not yours.'
Henry had no right to boss him around, thought
Peter. He'd been waiting such a long time for his turn.

Well, he wasn't waiting any longer. He'd start cutting out a window this minute.

Peter got out his scissors.

'Stop! It's a time machine, you toad!' shrieked Henry.

Peter paused.

Peter gasped.

Peter stared at the huge cardboard box. A time machine? *A time machine?* How could it be a time machine?

'It is not,' said Peter.

'Is too,' said Henry.

'But it's made of cardboard,' said Peter. 'And the washing machine came in it.'

Henry sighed.

'Don't you know anything? If it *looked* like a time machine everyone would try to steal it. It's a time machine in *disguise*.'

Peter looked at the time machine. On the one hand he didn't believe Henry for one minute. This was just one of Henry's tricks. Peter was a hundred million billion percent certain Henry was lying.

On the other hand, what if Henry *was* telling the truth for once and there was a real time machine in his sitting room?

'If it *is* a time machine I want to have a go,' said Peter.

'You can't. You're too young,' said Henry.

'Am not.'

'Are too.'

Perfect Peter stuck out his bottom lip.

'I don't believe you anyway.'

Horrid Henry was outraged.

'Okay, I'll prove it. I'll go to the future right now. Stand back. Don't move.'

Horrid Henry leapt into the box and closed the lid. The time machine began to shudder and shake.

Then everything was still for a very long time.

Perfect Peter didn't know what to do. What if Henry was gone – for ever? What if he were stuck in the future?

I could have his room, thought Peter. I could watch whatever I wanted on telly. I could –

Suddenly the box tipped over and Horrid Henry staggered out.

'Wh-wh- where am I?' he stuttered. Then he collapsed on the floor.

Peter stared at Henry.

Henry stared wildly at Peter.

'I've been to the future!' gasped Henry, panting. 'It was amazing. Wow. I met my great-great-great-grand-son. He still lives in this house. And he looks just like me.'

'So he's ugly,' muttered Peter.

'What – did – you – say?' hissed Henry.

'Nothing,' said Peter quickly. He didn't know what to think. 'Is this a trick, Henry?'

'Course it isn't,' said Henry. 'And just for that I won't let you have a go.'

'I can if I want to,' said Peter.

'You keep away from my time machine,' said Henry. 'One wrong move and you'll get blasted into the future.'

Perfect Peter walked a few steps towards the time machine. Then he paused.

'What's it like in the future?'

'Boys wear dresses,' said Horrid Henry. 'And lipstick. People talk Ugg language. *You'd* probably like it. Everyone just eats vegetables.'

'Really?'

'And kids have loads of homework.'

Perfect Peter loved homework.

'Ooohh.' This Peter *had* to see. Just in case Henry *was* telling the truth.

'I'm going to the future and you can't stop me,' said Peter.

'Go ahead,' said Henry. Then he snorted. 'You can't go looking like that!'

'Why not?' said Peter.

''Cause everyone will laugh at you.'

Perfect Peter hated people laughing at him.

'Why?'

'Because to them you'll look weird. Are you sure you really want to go to the future?'

'Yes,' said Peter.

'Are you sure you're sure?'

'YES,' said Peter.

'Then I'll get you ready,' said Henry solemnly.

'Thank you, Henry,' said Peter. Maybe he'd been wrong about Henry. Maybe going to the future had turned him into a nice brother.

Horrid Henry dashed out of the sitting room.

Perfect Peter felt a quiver of excitement. The future. What if Henry really was telling the truth?

Horrid Henry returned carrying a large wicker basket. He pulled out an old red dress of Mum's, some lipstick, and a black frothy drink.

'Here, put this on,' said Henry.

Perfect Peter put on the dress. It dragged onto the floor.

'Now, with a bit of lipstick,' said Horrid Henry,

applying big blobs of red lipstick all over Peter's face, 'you'll fit right in. Perfect,' he said, standing back to admire his handiwork. 'You look just like a boy from the future.'

'Okay,' said Perfect Peter.

'Now listen carefully,' said Henry. 'When you arrive, you won't be able to speak the language unless you drink this bibble babble drink. Take this with you and drink it when you get there.'

Henry held out the frothy black drink from his Dungeon Drink Kit. Peter took it.

'You can now enter the time machine.'

Peter obeyed. His heart was pounding.

'Don't get out until the time machine has stopped moving completely. Then count to twenty-five, and open the hatch very very slowly. You don't want a bit of you in the twenty-third century, and the rest here in the twenty-first. Good luck.'

Henry swirled the box round and round and round. Peter began to feel dizzy. The drink sloshed on the floor.

Then everything was still.

Peter's head was spinning. He counted to twenty-five, then crept out.

He was in the sitting room of a house that looked just like his. A boy wearing a bathrobe and silver waggly antennae with his face painted in blue stripes stood in front of him.

'Ugg?' said the strange boy.

'Henry?' said Peter.

'Uggg uggg bleuch ble bloop,' said the boy.

'Uggg uggg,' said Peter uncertainly.

'Uggh uggh drink ugggh,' said the boy, pointing to Peter's bibble babble drink.

Peter drank the few drops which were left.

'I'm Zog,' said Zog. 'Who are you?'

'I'm Peter,' said Peter.

'Ahhhhh! Welcome! You must be my great-great-great-uncle Peter. Your very nice brother Henry told me all about you when he visited me from the past.'

'Oh, what did he say?' said Peter.

'That you were an ugly toad.'

'I am not,' said Peter. 'Wait a minute,' he added suspiciously. 'Henry said that boys wore dresses in the future.'

'They do,' said Zog quickly. 'I'm a girl.'

'Oh,' said Peter. He gasped. Henry would *never* in a million years say he was a girl. Not even if he were being poked with red hot pokers. Could it be. . .

Peter looked around. 'This looks just like my sitting room.'

Zog snorted.

'Of course it does, Uncle Pete. This is now the Peter Museum. You're famous in the future. Everything has been kept exactly as it was.'

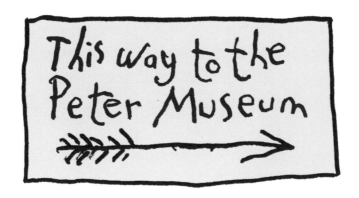

Peter beamed. He was famous in the future. He always knew he'd be famous. A Peter Museum! He couldn't wait to tell Spotless Sam and Tidy Ted.

There was just one more thing . . .

'What about Henry?' he asked. 'Is he famous too?'

'Nah,' said Zog smoothly. 'He's known as What's-His-Name, Peter's older brother.'

Ahh. Peter swelled with pride. Henry was in his lowly place, at last. That proved it. He'd really travelled to the future!

Peter looked out the window. Strange how the future didn't look so different from his own time.

Zog pointed.

'Our spaceships,' he announced.

Peter stared. Spaceships looked just like cars.

'Why aren't they flying?' said Peter.

'Only at night time,' said Zog. 'You can either drive 'em or fly 'em.'

'Wow,' said Peter.

'Don't *you* have spaceships?' said Zog.

'No,' said Peter. 'Cars.'

'I didn't know they had cars in olden days,' said Zog. 'Do you have blitzkatrons and zappersnappers?'

'No,' said Peter. 'What – '

The front door slammed. Mum walked in. She stared at Peter.

'What on earth. . .'

'Don't be scared,' said Peter. 'I'm Peter. I come from the past. I'm your great-great-great grandfather.'

Mum looked at Peter.

Peter looked at Mum.

'Why are you wearing my dress?' said Mum.

'It's not one of *yours*, silly,' said Peter. 'It belonged to my mum.'

'I see,' said Mum.

'Come on, Uncle Pete,' said Zog quickly, taking Peter firmly by the arm, 'I'll show you our supersonic hammock in the garden.'

'Okay, Zog,' said Peter happily.

Mum beamed.

'It's so lovely to see you playing nicely with your brother, Henry.'

Perfect Peter stood still.

'What did you call him?'

'Henry,' said Mum.

Peter felt a chill.

'So his name's not Zog? And he's not a girl?'

'Not the last time I looked,' said Mum.

'And this house isn't . . . the Peter Museum?'

Mum glared at Henry. 'Henry! Have you been teasing Peter again?'

'Ha ha tricked you!' shrieked Henry. 'Nah nah ne nah nah, wait till I tell everybody!'

'NO!' squealed Peter.

'NOOOOOOO!'

How *could* he have believed his horrible brother?

'Henry! You horrid boy! Go to your room! No TV for the rest of the day,' said Mum.

But Horrid Henry didn't care. The Mega-Mean Time Machine would go down in history as his greatest trick ever.

HOW TO BUILD YOUR OWN TIME MACHINE

1. Find huge box.
2. Load it with dials and gadgets.
3. Keep it away from grubby-fingered brothers and sisters.

Ugg Language Phrase Book

Uggg uggg bleuch ble bloop = Give me all your money

Uggga lugga = Wormy worm

Uggla mugla ugh? = Why are you so ugly?

Chgg uggggg = Chocolate

Ug mug ugguz lugga! = Out of my way, worm!

Ug mug ugguz tugga! = Out of my way, toad!

Uggla mugla ugh, lugga?

HORRiD HENRY'S PERFECT DAY

Henry was horrid.

Everyone said so, even his mother.

Henry threw food, Henry snatched, Henry pushed and shoved and pinched. Even his teddy, Mr Kill, avoided him when possible.

His parents despaired.

'What are we going to do about that horrid boy?' sighed Mum.

'How did two people as nice as us have such a horrid child?' sighed Dad.

When Horrid Henry's parents took Henry to school they walked behind him and pretended he was not theirs.

Children pointed at Henry and whispered to their parents, 'That's Horrid Henry.'

'He's the boy who threw my jacket in the mud.'

'He's the boy who squashed Billy's beetle.'

'He's the boy who . . .'

Fill in whatever terrible deed you like.

Horrid Henry was sure to have done it.

Horrid Henry had a younger
brother. His name was Perfect
Peter.

Perfect Peter always said 'Please'
and 'Thank you'. Perfect Peter
loved vegetables.

Perfect Peter always used a hankie
and never, ever picked his nose.

'Why can't you be perfect like
Peter?' said Henry's Mum every day.

As usual, Henry pretended not to
hear. He continued melting Peter's
crayons on the radiator.

But Horrid
Henry
started to
think.

'What
if *I* were perfect?' thought Henry.
'I wonder what would happen.'

When Henry woke the next
morning, he did not wake Peter
by pouring water on Peter's head.

Peter did not scream.

This meant Henry's parents overslept and Henry and Peter were late for Cubs.

Henry was very happy.

Peter was very sad to be late for Cubs.

But because he was perfect, Peter did not whine or complain.

On the way to Cubs Henry did not squabble with Peter over who sat in front. He did not pinch Peter and he did not shove Peter.

Back home, when Perfect Peter built a castle, Henry did not knock it down. Instead, Henry sat on the sofa and read a book.

Mum and Dad ran into the room.

'It's awfully quiet in here,' said Mum. 'Are you being horrid, Henry?'

'No,' said Henry.

'Peter, is Henry knocking your castle down?'

Peter longed to say 'yes'. But that would be a lie.

'No,' said Peter.

He wondered why Henry was behaving so strangely.

'What are you doing, Henry?' said Dad.

'Reading a wonderful story about some super mice,' said Henry.

Dad had never seen Henry read a book before. He checked to see if a comic was hidden inside.

There was no comic. Henry was actually reading a book.

'Hmmmm,' said Dad.

It was almost time for dinner. Henry was hungry and went into the kitchen where Dad was cooking.

But instead of shouting, 'I'm starving! Where's my food?' Henry said, 'Dad, you look tired. Can I help get supper ready?'

'Don't be horrid, Henry,' said Dad, pouring peas into boiling water. Then he stopped.

'What did you say, Henry?' asked Dad.

'Can *I* help, Dad?' said Perfect Peter.

'I asked if you needed any help,' said Henry.

'I asked first,' said Peter.

'Henry will just make a mess,' said Dad. 'Peter, would you peel the carrots while I sit down for a moment?'

'Of course,' said Perfect Peter.

Peter washed his spotless hands.

Peter put on his spotless apron.

Peter rolled up his spotless sleeves.

Peter waited for Henry to snatch the peeler.

But Henry laid the table instead.

Mum came into the kitchen.

'Smells good,' she said. 'Thank you, darling Peter, for laying the table. What a good boy you are.'

Peter did not say anything.

'I laid the table, Mum,' said Henry.

Mum stared at him.

'You?' said Mum.

'Me,' said Henry.

'Why?' said Mum.

Henry smiled.

'To be helpful,' he said.

'You've done something horrid, haven't you, Henry?' said Dad.

'No,' said Henry. He tried to look sweet.

'I'll lay the table tomorrow,' said Perfect Peter.

'Thank you, angel,' said Mum.

'Dinner is ready,' said Dad.

The family sat down at the table.

Dinner was spaghetti and meatballs with peas and carrots.

Henry ate his dinner with his knife and fork and spoon.

He did not throw peas at Peter and he did not slurp.

He did not chew with his mouth open and he did not slouch.

'Sit properly, Henry,' said Dad.

'I am sitting properly,' said Henry.

Dad looked up from his plate. He looked surprised.

'So you are,' he said.

Perfect Peter could not eat. Why wasn't Henry throwing peas at him?

Peter's hand reached slowly for a pea.

When no one was looking, he flicked the pea at Henry.

'Ouch,' said Henry.

'Don't be horrid, Henry,' said Mum.

Henry reached for a fistful of peas. Then Henry remembered he was being perfect and stopped.

Peter smiled and waited. But no peas bopped him on the head.

Perfect Peter did not understand. Where was the foot that always kicked him under the table?

Slowly, Peter stretched out his foot and kicked Henry.

'OUCH,' said Henry.

'Don't be horrid, Henry,' said Dad.

'But I . . .' said Henry, then stopped.

Henry's foot wanted to kick Perfect Peter round the block. Then Henry remembered he was being perfect and continued to eat.

'You're very quiet tonight, Henry,' said Dad.

'The better to enjoy my lovely dinner,' said Henry.

'Henry, where are your peas and carrots?' asked Mum.

'I ate them,' said Henry. 'They were delicious.'

Mum looked on the floor. She looked under Henry's chair. She looked under his plate.

'You ate your peas and carrots?' said Mum slowly. She felt Henry's forehead.

'Are you feeling all right, Henry?'

'Yeah,' said Horrid Henry. 'I'm fine, thank you for asking,' he added quickly.

Mum and Dad looked at each other. What was going on?

Then they looked at Henry.

'Henry, come here and let me give you a big kiss,'
said Mum. 'You are a wonderful boy. Would you like a
piece of fudge cake?'

Peter interrupted.

'No cake for me, thank you,' said Peter. 'I would
rather have more vegetables.'

Henry let himself be
kissed. Oh my, it was
hard work being
perfect.

He smiled sweetly
at Peter.

'I would love some cake, thank you,' said Henry.

Perfect Peter could stand it no longer. He picked up his plate and aimed at Henry.

Then Peter threw the spaghetti.

Henry ducked.

Splat!

Spaghetti landed on Mum's head. Tomato sauce trickled down her neck and down her new blue fuzzy jumper.

'Peter!!!!'

yelled Mum and Dad.

'YOU HORRID BOY!' yelled Mum.

'GO TO YOUR ROOM!!' yelled Dad.

Perfect Peter burst into tears and ran to his room.

Mum wiped spaghetti off her face. She looked very funny.

Henry tried not to laugh. He squeezed his lips together tightly.

But it was no use. He could not stop a laugh escaping.

'It's not funny!' shouted Dad.

'Go to your room!' shouted Mum.

But Henry didn't care.

Who would have thought being perfect would be such fun?

HORRID HENRY'S PERFECT DAY DIARY

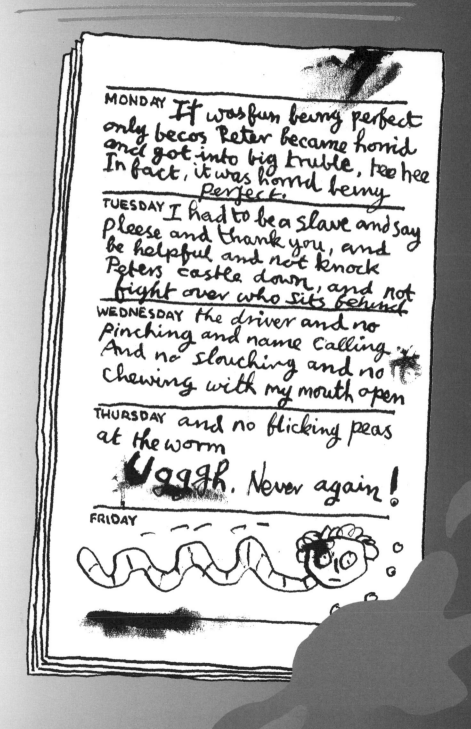

MONDAY It was fun being perfect only becos Peter became horrid and got into big truble, hee hee In fact, it was horrid being perfect.

TUESDAY I had to be a slave and say pleese and thank you, and be helpful and not knock Peters castle down, and not fight over who sits behind

WEDNESDAY the driver and no pinching and name calling. And no slouching and no chewing with my mouth open

THURSDAY and no flicking peas at the worm **Ugggh.** Never again!

FRIDAY

PERFECT PETER'S HORRID DAY

'Henry, use your fork!' said Dad.

'*I'm* using my fork,' said Peter.

'Henry, sit down!' said Mum.

'*I'm* sitting down,' said Peter.

'Henry, stop spitting!' said Dad.

'*I'm* not spitting!' said Peter.

'Henry, chew with your mouth shut!' said Mum.

'*I'm* chewing with my mouth shut!' said Peter.

'Henry, don't make a mess!' said Dad.

'*I'm* not making a mess,' said Peter.

'What?' said Mum.

Perfect Peter was not having a perfect day.

Mum and Dad are too busy yelling at Henry all the time to notice how good *I* am, thought Peter.

When was the last time Mum and Dad had said, 'Marvellous, Peter, you're using your fork!'

'WONDERFUL, Peter, you're sitting down!'

'SUPERB, Peter, you're not spitting!'

'FABULOUS, Peter, you're chewing with your mouth shut!'

'PERFECT, Peter, you never make a mess!'

Perfect Peter dragged himself upstairs.

Everyone just expects me to be perfect, thought Peter, as he wrote his Aunt Ruby a thank you note for the super thermal vests. It's not fair.

From downstairs came the sound of raised voices.

'Henry, get your muddy shoes off the sofa!' yelled Dad.

'Henry, stop being so horrid!' yelled Mum.

Then Perfect Peter started to think.

What if *I* were horrid? thought Peter.

Peter's mouth dropped open. What a horrid thought! He looked around quickly, to see if anyone had noticed.

He was alone in his immaculate bedroom. No one would ever know he'd thought such a terrible thing.

But imagine being horrid. No, that would never do.

Peter finished his letter, read a few pages of his favourite magazine, *Best Boy*, got into bed and turned off his light without being asked.

Imagine being horrid.

What *if* I were horrid, thought Peter. I wonder what would happen?

When Peter woke up the next morning, he did not dash downstairs to get breakfast ready. Instead, he lazed in bed for an extra five minutes.

When he finally got out of bed Peter did not straighten the duvet.

Nor did Peter plump his pillows.

Instead Peter looked at his tidy bedroom and had a very wicked thought.

Quickly, before he could change his mind, he took off his pyjama top and did not fold it neatly. Instead he dropped it on the floor.

Mum came in.

'Good morning, darling. You must be tired, sleeping in.'

Peter hoped Mum would notice his untidy room.

But Mum did not say anything.

'Notice anything, Mum?' said Peter.

Mum looked around.

'No,' said Mum.

'Oh,' said Peter.

'What?' said Mum.

'I haven't made my bed,' said Peter.

'Clever you to remember it's washday,' said Mum. She stripped the sheets and duvet cover, then swooped and picked up Peter's pyjama top.

'Thank you, dear,' said Mum. She smiled and left.

Peter frowned. Clearly, he would need to work harder at being horrid.

He looked at his beautifully arranged books.

'No!' he gasped, as a dreadful thought sneaked into his head.

Then Peter squared his shoulders. Today was his horrid day, and horrid he would be. He went up to his books and knocked them over.

'HENRY!' bellowed Dad. 'Get up this minute!'

Henry slumped past Peter's door.

Peter decided he would call Henry a horrid name.

'Hello, Ugly,' said Peter. Then he went wild and stuck out his tongue.

Henry marched into Peter's bedroom. He glared at Peter.

'What did you call me?' said Henry.

Peter screamed.

Mum ran into the room.

'Stop being horrid, Henry! Look what a mess you've made in here!'

'He called me Ugly,' said Henry.

'Of course he didn't,' said Mum.

'He did too,' said Henry.

'Peter never calls people names,' said Mum. 'Now pick up those books you knocked over.'

'I didn't knock them over,' said Henry.

'Well, who did, then, the man in the moon?' said Mum.

Henry pointed at Peter.

'He did,' said Henry.

'*Did* you, Peter?' asked Mum.

Peter wanted to be really really horrid and tell a lie. But he couldn't.

'I did it, Mum,' said Peter. Boy, would he get told off now.

'Don't be silly, of course you didn't,' said Mum. 'You're just saying that to protect Henry.'

Mum smiled at Peter and frowned at Henry.

'Now leave Peter alone and get dressed,' said Mum.

'But it's the weekend,' said Henry.

'So?' said Mum.

'But Peter's not dressed.'

'I'm sure he was just about to get dressed before you barged in,' said Mum. 'See? He's already taken his pyjama top off.'

'I don't want to get dressed,' said Peter boldly.

'You poor boy,' said Mum. 'You must be feeling ill. Pop back into bed and I'll bring your breakfast up. Just let me put some clean sheets on.'

Perfect Peter scowled a tiny scowl. Clearly, he wasn't very good at being horrid yet. He would have to try harder.

At lunch Peter ate pasta with his fingers. No one noticed.

Then Henry scooped up pasta with both fists and slurped some into his mouth.

'Henry! Use your fork!' said Dad. Peter spat into his plate.

'Peter, are you choking?' said Dad.

Henry spat across the table.

'Henry! Stop that disgusting spitting this instant!' said Mum.

Peter chewed with his mouth open.

'Peter, is there something wrong with your teeth?' asked Mum.

Henry chomped and dribbled and gulped with his mouth as wide open as possible.

'Henry! This is your last warning. Keep your mouth shut when you eat!' shouted Dad.

Peter did not understand. Why didn't anyone notice how horrid he was? He stretched out his foot and kicked Henry under the table.

Henry kicked him back harder.

Peter shrieked.

Henry got told off. Peter got dessert.

Perfect Peter did not know what to do. No matter how hard he tried to be horrid, nothing seemed to work.

'Now boys,' said Mum, 'Grandma is coming for tea this afternoon. Please keep the house tidy and leave the chocolates alone.'

'What chocolates?' said Henry.

'Never you mind,' said Mum. 'You'll have some when Grandma gets here.'

Then Peter had a truly stupendously horrid idea. He left the table without waiting to be excused and sneaked into the sitting room.

Peter searched high. Peter searched low. Then Peter found a large box of chocolates hidden behind some books.

Peter opened the box. Then he took a tiny bite out of every single chocolate. When he found good ones with gooey chocolate fudge centres he ate them. The yucky raspberry and strawberry and lemon creams he put back.

Hee hee, thought Peter. He felt excited. What he had done was absolutely awful. Mum and Dad were sure to notice.

Then Peter looked round the tidy sitting room. Why not mess it up a bit?

Peter grabbed a cushion from the sofa. He was just about to fling it on the floor when he heard someone sneaking into the room.

'What are you doing?' said Henry.

'Nothing, Ugly,' said Peter.

'Don't call me Ugly, Toad,' said Henry.

'Don't call me Toad, Ugly,' said Peter.

'Toad!'

'Ugly!'

'TOAD!'

'UGLY!'

Mum and Dad ran in.

'Henry!' shouted Dad. 'Stop being horrid!'

'I'm not being horrid!' said Henry. 'Peter's calling me names.'

Mum and Dad looked at each other. What was going on?

'Don't lie, Henry,' said Mum.

'I did call him a name, Mum,' said Peter. 'I called him Ugly because he is ugly. So there.'

Mum stared at Peter.

Dad stared at Peter.

Henry stared at Peter.

'If Peter did call you a name, it's because you called him one first,' said Mum. 'Now leave Peter alone.'

Mum and Dad left.

'Serves you right, Henry,' said Peter.

'You're very strange today,' said Henry.

'No I'm not,' said Peter.

'Oh yes you are,' said Henry. 'You can't fool me. Listen, want to play a trick on Grandma?'

'No!' said Peter.

Ding dong.

'Grandma's here!' called Dad.

Mum, Dad, Henry, Peter and Grandma sat down together in the sitting room.

'Let me take your bag, Grandma,' said Henry sweetly.

'Thank you dear,' said Grandma.

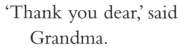

When no one was looking Henry took Grandma's glasses out of her bag and hid them behind Peter's cushion.

Mum and Dad passed around tea and home-made biscuits on the best china plates.

Peter sat on the edge of the sofa and held his breath.

Any second now Mum would get out the box of half-eaten chocolates.

Mum stood up and got the box.

'Peter, would you like to pass round the chocolates?' said Mum.

'Okay,' said Peter. His knees felt wobbly. Everyone was about to find out what a horrid thing he had done.

Peter held out the box.

'Would you like a chocolate, Mum?' said Peter. His heart pounded.

'No thanks,' said Mum.

'What about me?' said Henry.

'Would you like a chocolate, Dad?' said Peter. His hands shook.

'No thanks,' said Dad.

'What about me!' said Henry.

'Shh, Henry,' said Mum. 'Don't be so rude.'

'Would you like a chocolate, Grandma?' said Peter.

There was no escape now. Grandma loved chocolates.

'Yes, please!' said Grandma. She peered closely into the box. 'Let me see, what shall I choose? Now, where are my specs?'

Grandma reached into her bag and fumbled about.

'That's funny,' said Grandma. 'I was sure I'd brought them. Never mind.'

Grandma reached into the box, chose a chocolate and popped it into her mouth.

'Oh,' said Grandma. 'Strawberry cream. Go on, Peter, have a chocolate.'

'No thanks,' said Peter.

'WHAT ABOUT ME!' screamed Horrid Henry.

'None for you,' said Dad. 'That's not how you ask.'

Peter gritted his teeth. If no one was going to notice the chewed chocolates he'd have to do it himself.

'I will have a chocolate,' announced Peter loudly. 'Hey! Who's eaten all the fudge ones? And who's taken bites out of the rest?'

'Henry!' yelled Mum. 'I've told you a million times to leave the chocolates alone!'

'It wasn't me!' said Henry. 'It was Peter!'

'Stop blaming Peter,' said Dad.

'You know he never eats sweets.'

'It's not fair!' shrieked Henry. Then he snatched the box from Peter. 'I want some CHOCOLATES!'

Peter snatched it back. The open box fell to the floor. Chocolates flew everywhere.

'HENRY, GO TO YOUR ROOM!' yelled Mum.

'IT'S NOT FAIR!' screeched Henry. 'I'll get you for this Peter!'

Then Horrid Henry ran out of the room, slamming the door behind him.

Grandma patted the sofa beside her. Peter sat down. He could not believe it. What did a boy have to do to get noticed?

'How's my best boy?' asked Grandma.

Peter sighed.

Grandma gave him a big hug. 'You're the best boy in the world, Peter, did you know that?'

Peter glowed. Grandma was right! He was the best.

But wait. Today he was horrid.

NO! He was perfect. His horrid day was over.

He was much happier being perfect, anyway. Being horrid was horrible.

I've had my horrid day, thought Peter. Now I can be perfect again.

What a marvellous idea. Peter smiled and leaned back against the cushion.

CRUNCH!

'Oh dear,' said Grandma. 'That sounds like my specs. I wonder how they got there.'

Mum looked at Peter.

Dad looked at Peter.

'It wasn't me!' said Peter.

'Of course not,' said Grandma. 'I must have dropped them. Silly me.'

'Hmmmm,' said Dad.

Perfect Peter ran into the kitchen and looked about. Now that I'm perfect again, what good deeds can I do? he thought.

Then Peter noticed all the dirty tea cups and plates piled up on the worktop. He had never done the washing up all by himself before. Mum and Dad would be so pleased.

Peter carefully washed and dried all the dishes.

Then he stacked them up and carried them to the cupboard.

'BOOOOOOO!'

shrieked Horrid Henry, leaping out from behind the door.

Henry vanished.

Mum and Dad ran in.

The best china lay in pieces all over the floor.

'Peter!!!!'

yelled Mum and Dad.

'YOU HORRID BOY!' yelled Mum.

'GO TO YOUR ROOM!' yelled Dad.

'But . . . But . . .' gasped Peter.

'NO BUTS!' shouted Mum. 'GO! Oh, my lovely dishes!'

Perfect Peter ran to his room.

'AHHHHHHHHHHHH!'

shrieked Peter.

PERFECT PETER'S DIARY

It was boring being horrid.
I had to eat chocolate, mess up
my room, eat with my fingers,
chew with my mouth open,
and leave the table without
being excused.
I even tried to tell a lie.
Never again!

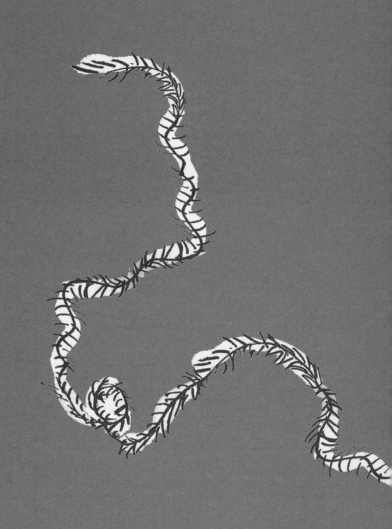

HORRiD HENRY'S CHRISTMAS PRESENTS

Horrid Henry sat by the Christmas tree and stuffed himself full of the special sweets he'd nicked from the special Christmas Day stash when Mum and Dad weren't looking. After his triumph in the school Christmas play, Horrid Henry was feeling delighted with himself and with the world.

Granny and Grandpa, his grown-up cousins Pimply Paul and Prissy Polly, and their baby Vomiting Vera were coming to spend Christmas. Whoopee, thought Horrid Henry, because they'd all have to bring *him* presents. Thankfully, Rich Aunt Ruby and Stuck-Up Steve weren't coming. They were off skiing. Henry hadn't forgotten the dreadful lime green cardigan Aunt Ruby had given him last year. And much as he hated cousin Polly, anyone was better than Stuck-Up Steve, even someone who squealed all the time and had a baby who threw up on everyone.

Mum dashed into the sitting room, wearing a flour-covered apron and looking frantic. Henry choked down his mouthful of sweets.

'Right, who wants to decorate the tree?' said Mum. She held out a cardboard box brimming with tinsel and gold and silver and blue baubles.

'Me!' said Henry.

'Me!' said Peter.

Horrid Henry dashed to the box and scooped up as many shiny ornaments as he could.

'I want to put on the gold baubles,' said Henry.

'I want to put on the tinsel,' said Peter.

'Keep away from my side of the tree,' hissed Henry.

'You don't have a side,' said Peter.

'Do too.'

'Do not,' said Peter.

'I want to put on the tinsel *and* the baubles,' said Henry.

'But I want to do the tinsel,' said Peter.

'Tough,' said Henry, draping Peter in tinsel.

'Muuum!' wailed Peter. 'Henry's hogging all the decorations! And he's putting tinsel on me.'

'Don't be horrid, Henry,' said Mum. 'Share with your brother.'

Peter carefully wrapped blue tinsel round the lower branches.

'Don't put it there,' said Henry, yanking it off. Trust Peter to ruin his beautiful plan.

'MUUUM!' wailed Peter.

'He's wrecking my design,' screeched Henry. 'He doesn't know how to decorate a tree.'

'But I wanted it there!' protested Peter. 'Leave my tinsel alone.'

'You leave my stuff alone then,' said Henry.

'He's wrecked my design!' shrieked Henry and Peter.

'Stop fighting, both of you!' shrieked Mum.

'He started it!' screamed Henry.

'Did not!'

'Did too!'

'That's enough,' said Mum. 'Now, whose turn is it to put the fairy on top?'

'I don't want to have that stupid fairy,' wailed Horrid Henry. 'I want to have Terminator Gladiator instead.'

'No,' said Peter. 'I want the fairy. We've always had the fairy.'

'Terminator!'

'Fairy!'

'TERMINATOR!'

'FAIRY!'

Slap Slap

'WAAAAAAA!'

'We're having the fairy,' said Mum firmly, 'and *I'll* put it on the tree.'

'NOOOOOOO!'

screamed Henry. 'Why can't we do what I want to do? I never get to have what I want.'

'Liar!' whimpered Peter.

'I've had enough of this,' said Mum. 'Now get your presents and put them under the tree.'

Peter ran off.

Henry stood still.

'Henry,' said Mum. 'Have you finished wrapping your Christmas presents?'

Yikes, thought Horrid Henry. What am I going to

do now? The moment he'd been dreading for weeks had arrived.

'Henry! I'm not going to ask you again,' said Mum. 'Have you finished wrapping all your Christmas presents?'

'Yes!' bellowed Horrid Henry.

This was not entirely true. Henry had not finished wrapping his Christmas presents. In fact, he hadn't even started. The truth was, Henry had finished wrapping because he had no presents to wrap.

This was certainly *not* his fault. He *had* bought a few gifts, certainly. He knew Peter would love the box of green Day-Glo slime. And if he didn't, well, he knew who to give it to. And Granny and Grandpa and Mum and Dad and Paul and Polly would have adored the big boxes of chocolates Henry had won at the school fair. Could he help it if the chocolates had called his name so loudly that he'd been forced to eat them all? And

then Granny had been complaining about gaining weight. Surely it would have been very unkind to give her chocolate. And eating chocolate would have just made Pimply Paul's pimples worse. Henry'd done him a big favour eating that box.

And it was hardly Henry's fault when he'd needed extra goo for a raid on the Secret Club and Peter's present was the only stuff to hand. He'd *meant* to buy replacements. But he had so many things he needed to buy for himself that when he opened his skeleton bank to get out some cash for Christmas shopping, only 35p had rolled out.

'I've bought and wrapped all *my* presents, Mum,' said Perfect Peter. 'I've been saving my pocket money for months.'

'Whoopee for you,' said Henry.

'Henry, it's always better to give than to receive,' said Peter.

Mum beamed. 'Quite right, Peter.'

'Says who?' growled Horrid Henry. 'I'd much rather *get* presents.'

'Don't be so horrid, Henry,' said Mum.

'Don't be so selfish, Henry,' said Dad.

Horrid Henry stuck out his tongue. Mum and Dad gasped.

'You horrid boy,' said Mum.

'I just hope Father Christmas didn't see that,' said Dad.

'Henry,' said Peter, 'Father Christmas won't bring you any presents if you're bad.'

'AAARRRGGHHH!'

Horrid Henry sprang at Peter. He was a grizzly bear guzzling a juicy morsel.

'AAAAIIEEE,' wailed Peter. 'Henry pinched me.'

'Henry! Go to your room,' said Mum.

'Fine!' screamed Horrid Henry, stomping off and slamming the door. Why did he get stuck with the world's meanest and most horrible parents? *They* certainly didn't deserve any presents.

Presents! Why couldn't he just *get* them? Why oh why did he have to *give* them? Giving other people presents was such a waste of his hard-earned money. Every time he gave a present it meant something he couldn't buy for himself. Goodbye chocolate. Goodbye comics. Goodbye Deluxe Goo-Shooter. And then, if you bought anything good, it was so horrible having to give it away. He'd practically cried having to give Ralph that Terminator Gladiator poster for his birthday. And the Mutant Max lunchbox Mum made him give Kasim still made him gnash his teeth whenever he saw Kasim with it.

Now he was stuck, on Christmas Eve, with no money, and no presents to give anyone, deserving or not.

And then Henry had a wonderful, spectacular idea. It was so wonderful, and so spectacular, that he couldn't believe he hadn't thought of it before. Who said he had to *buy* presents? Didn't Mum and Dad always say it was the *thought* that counted? And oh boy was he thinking.

Granny was sure to love a Mutant Max comic. After all, who wouldn't? Then when she'd finished enjoying it, he could borrow it back. Horrid Henry rummaged under his bed and found a recent copy. In fact, it would be a shame if Grandpa got jealous of Granny's great present. Safer to give them each one, thought Henry, digging deep into his pile to find one with the fewest torn pages.

Now let's see, Mum and Dad. He could draw them a lovely picture. Nah, that would take too long. Even better, he could write them a poem.

Henry sat down at his desk, grabbed a pencil, and wrote:

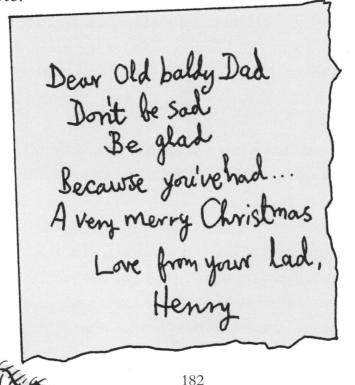

Dear Old baldy Dad
Don't be sad
Be glad
Because you've had...
A very merry Christmas
Love from your lad,
Henry

Not bad, thought Henry. Not bad. And so cheap!
Now one for Mum.

Dear Old wrinkly Mum
Don't be glum
Cause you've got a fat tum
And an even bigger bum
Ho ho ho hum
Love from your son,
Henry

Wow! It was hard finding so many words to rhyme
with *Mum* but he'd done it. And the poem was nice
and Christmassy with the 'ho ho ho'. *Son* didn't rhyme
but hopefully Mum wouldn't notice because she'd be
so thrilled with the rest of the poem. When he was
famous she'd be proud to show off the poem her son
had written specially for her.

Now, Polly. Hmmmn. She was always squeaking and
squealing about dirt and dust. Maybe a lovely kitchen
sponge? Or a rag she could use to mop up after Vera?

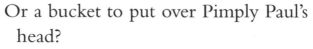

Or a bucket to put over Pimply Paul's head?

Wait. What about some soap?

Horrid Henry nipped into the bathroom. Yes! There was a tempting bar of blue soap going to waste in the soap dish by the bathtub. True, it had been used once or twice, but a bit of smoothing with his fingers would sort that out. In fact, Polly and Paul could share this present, it was such a good one.

Whistling, Horrid Henry wrapped up the soap in sparkling reindeer paper. He was a genius. Why hadn't he ever done this before? And a lovely rag from under the sink would be perfect as a gag for Vera.

That just left Peter and all his present problems would be over. A piece of chewing gum, only one careful owner? A collage of sweet wrappers which spelled out *Worm*? The unused comb Peter had given *him* last Christmas?

Aha. Peter loved bunnies. What better present than a picture of a bunny?

It was the work of a few moments for Henry to draw a bunny and slash a few blue lines across it to colour it in. Then he signed his name in big letters at the bottom. Maybe he should be a famous artist and not a poet when he grew up, he thought, admiring his handiwork. Henry had heard that artists got paid loads of cash just for stacking a few bricks or hurling paint at a white canvas. Being an artist sounded like a great job, since it left so much time for playing computer games.

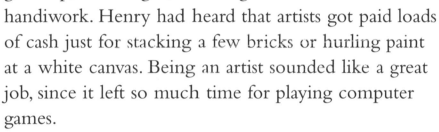

Horrid Henry dumped his presents beneath the Christmas tree and sighed happily. This was one Christmas where he was sure to get a lot more than he gave.

Whoopee!

Who could ask for anything more?

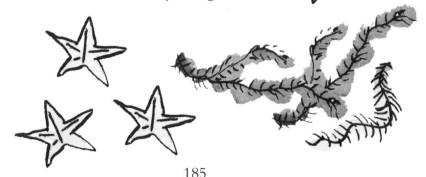

HORRID HENRY'S GIFT IDEAS

It's **NEVER** better to give than to receive. Spending hard-earned cash on presents for undeserving people is

Certificates

Henry.

Sweet wrapper collage

me by me

the worst part about Christmas. Remember, it's the thought that counts. And thoughts don't count.

Henry
Henry
Henry
Henry
Henry
Henry

My autograph

Drawings of me

Miss Battleaxe
Henry

Rain
Henry

Peter
Henry

a black hole
Henry

a pet worm
Henry

Drawings

A plastic bag (very useful)

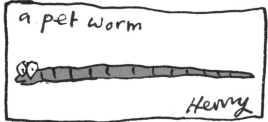

HORRiD HENRY'S FAMILY FACT FILE
(All the stuff they don't want anyone to know!!!)

Secret Dreams

Henry: to be a dictator and rule the world

*

Peter: to marry Miss Lovely

*

Mum: to be a tap dancer

Dad: to be a Rock'n'Roll god

*

Aunt Ruby: to be best friends with the Queen

*

Stuck-up Steve: to be a champion skier

*

Fluffy: to live in a house filled with mice

*

Fang: to be bigger than Fluffy

Deepest, Darkest Secrets

Mum: she sneaks sweets from the sweet jar

*

Dad: he is scared of injections

*

Peter: Miss Lovely once told him off for running in class

Stuck-up Steve: he can't sleep without Little Ducky

*

Henry: wouldn't you like to know!

189

HORRiD HENRY

by Francesca Simon

Illustrated by Tony Ross

Paperbacks with four stories each

Big colour collections

HORRID HENRY'S BIG BAD BOOK
HORRID HENRY'S EVIL ENEMIES
HORRID HENRY'S WICKED WAYS
HORRID HENRY RULES THE WORLD

Extra books

HORRID HENRY'S JOKE BOOK
HORRID HENRY'S JOLLY JOKE BOOK
HORRID HENRY'S MIGHTY JOKE BOOK

For younger readers

DON'T BE HORRID, HENRY!

All the storybooks are available on
CD, read by Miranda Richardson